AF538901

*For my parents*

*Content*

# *Author's Note*

The title of this collection of stories came to me one evening when I was sitting under a tree, mulling over the possibilities. I was trying to think of something that would encompass them in their entirety that would fit their individual characteristics, while not taking away from their wholeness. I finally decided upon the Wych Stories. It appealed to my imagination and gave life to the creative form of the stories completely.

Wych is an Eurasian elm tree, which has round and long pointed leaves, clusters of small flowers and winged fruits. The abundance points to fertility, life and dare I say it – imagination. I hope I do not appear too arrogant when I liken myself to the tree and the stories and the abundant types of stories as represented by the leaves, the fruits and the flowers.

The stories in this collection fall into two main categories. One that deals with real life situations, the day-to-day occurrences we all go through. Issues such as prostitution, marital insecurities, the dreaded disease AIDS social snobbishness and even old age. I have always been interested in life's many vignettes and am glad that I have had an opportunity to delve deeper, in a sense to put them under a microscope and see what they are all about.

The second category deals with the surreal. These stories are imaginative, even uncanny. They have to do with the mind and the way it works under stress, when faced with the unknown or even when it shuts out reality and forms a world of its own where unreal experiences take place. The unknown has always fascinated me. An early induction into the works of Roald Dahl had me hooked.

Unlike my first novel Kindred Spirits which quite literally appeared out of nowhere and transformed itself on paper, these stories have been with me for a long time. Right from their inception through to fruition, we have been companions. It has been an interesting journey, for along with the stories I too have grown, have changed, have questioned.

Wych or witch, which is the other way to spell it, also refers to that species from ancient folk-lore who, according to popular belief, cast her spells upon a vulnerable humanity. I prefer to see her in another light. She creates her own magic and invites the reader to enter her world. It is strange, it is individual but it is also exciting and arouses differing perceptions. Come, enter this world and partake of the witch's wych stories!

A short story occurs, in the imaginative sense. To write one is to try to express from a situation in the exterior or interior world the life-giving drop – sweat, tear, semen, saliva – that will spread an intensity on the page, burn a hole in it.

*Nadine Gordimer*

# 1

# Saurian

It was staring at me through eyes that were wide and unblinking. It was poised intent on movement, any second it would be gone in a flash, across the ceiling to hide in some corner out of my sight. But at the moment it was waiting to see what I would do. Would I try to bring it down and take its life or would I let it be. There would always be another one - what did it matter?

The yellowish mustard tinge of its skin was stark against the white of the walls and the stunted tail stood further pronounced. The tail had probably got caught in some window or crevice or perhaps bitten off by a fellow mate. There were many lizards in the house, indeed in such an old bungalow as ours they came out from every nook and corner in the summer months. They descended upon us every year en masse and on each sojourn with more visitors than the previous time. As I picked up my briefcase to leave for my trip, my companion of a few minutes scuttled across the ceiling and disappeared from my view.

It was late, well passed the bewitching hour when I got home. The light by the gate flickered in solitary splendour. The driveway looked dull and depressing, most of the lights had been switched off and I grimaced as I realized we were conserving electricity like everyone else during the sweltering summer months.

There were dark shadows everywhere where the lonely light failed to penetrate and I hurried out of the car, never one to linger in such darkness for longer than it was necessary.

As I walked into the house, I encountered a similar darkness. There was one table lamp on in the corridor that provided less light and more shadows and because of the low voltage looked altogether too depressing. I was extremely tired having spent a major part of the day with the irate customers, who were obnoxiously difficult to please. And coupled with a crack of dawn awakening and the tiring journey, I was completely and utterly exhausted.

I went to the kitchen and took a chilled beer out of the fridge. As I dark thirstily, I rummaged through the other contents to see if there was anything appetizing to eat. Although I had a substantial breakfast in anticipation of a good business deal, lunch had been a dismal affair and my appetite had all but wanted at that point, although my clients had eaten heartily at my expense. Dinner had not seemed to matter somewhat earlier but now I was ravenous. I found half a roast chicken, some creamy mint and spring onion potato salad and half a baguette which I heated to perfection in the oven. I sat down in front of the television and devoured the lot. I have to confess it was a delicious meal and I enjoyed every morsel. Till that moment, I had not bothered to see if Meera was awake. My traveling all over the country and arriving home like a nocturnal visitor was something she had become used to over the years. So she would definitely not be awake. Why should she be, I asked myself? It would have been most unusual.

Now as I walked up the stairs towards the bedroom, I was quite surprised to see all the lights on. This indicated that she was awake. Of course I had no idea and neither had she that I was back home. Indeed the house was built in such a manner that the bedrooms were cut off to ensure privacy. So there was no way I could have known she was awake unless I actually came to the bedroom.

Immediately my heart beat accelerated. Something had to be wrong, otherwise why would the lights be on and why was there no sound? I walked into the bedroom as fast as my scared appehension would allow. There was no one in the bedroom. A quick glance heralded no one in sight. And then I did a double slow check just to make sure.

I steeled myself to look at each corner in the bedroom calmly, the dressing room, the chaise lounge, but no, there was no doubt about it. She was not in the bedroom. "Meera, Meera, where are you? Where are you?", I shouted loudly.

Silence and bright lights greeted my outburst and seemed all the more dismaying in the dead of the night. I rushed towards the bathroom as an afterthought. She couldn't be there and not have responded. She would certainly have heard me shouting from the bedroom. I heaved myself against the door. It was locked. I turned the door knob several times but it refused to budge. There was no doubt about it. The door was locked from the inside.

For a brief moment I was amazed. That must mean Meena was inside. Oh my God, oh my God. I started to panic. Something must be terribly wrong for her not to answer. Maybe she had slipped on the granite floor and broken a bone. She must have lost consciousness. Even if she had hurt herself, she would have made some noise to show that she was aware that I was back home. She could have banged the door.... Hit on the walls ... anything. But there was nothing except me and eerie silence of the night.

I twisted the knob which was a solid contraption of pure brass, this way and that way but to no avail. I tried to open the door by pushing my quite inconsiderable weight against it but the door refused to budge just as I knew it wouldn't. But I was not in a rational state of mind to think of the logicality of my action. All I knew was that I just had to do something.

I rushed out to the bedroom past the balcony and hurried through the kitchen and the garden to the back part of the house. Since it was a bungalow, we often left the bathroom door open for the servants to clean. This way they need not have access to the rest of the house. I had always found it a great convenience. I prayed it was still open. "Please let it be open, please let it be open," I mumbled to myself out loud.

I ran straight up to the door and crashed against it with all my might hoping to find myself inside the bathroom. But I only succeeded in bruising my shoulder. As I bit my lip in agony, I tried to push open the door once again. It wouldn't move. It was locked. I stood helpless for a moment and could not help noticing the proliferation of lizards scuttling up and down the wall; busy, busy, busy. Busy doing what I had never really understood. There was also a hoard of insects so perhaps they were all getting ready for a feast. As I pushed against the door one of the lizards dropped on my hand, plop – it was there for one infinitesimal moment – and then was gone in a flash.

It was so temporary, so fleeting. But I was caught unawares. Both the suddenness of the situation and the unpleasant sensation left me screaming. I finally calmed down but by now I was positively hysterical. I longed to have a bath and wash myself thoroughly, especially my hand where the lizard had perched for that infinitesimal moment. But I knew it as not to be. Or at least not yet.

"Meera, open the door. Please open the door. Are you all right? Can you hear me? Can you hear me?" Again I pushed and heaved my body against the door. This particular door had no key lock and I was hoping that the latch would eventually succumb under my constant battering. But at that moment the door stood as invincible as before.

I rushed back inside, almost snuffing out the lives of two lizards who were zooming across my path at a high speed.

Who, I thought to myself, who could help? I picked up the telephone but could not remember any numbers though I always prided on my keen memory. Just one thought kept going through my head. What should I do, I hope Meera is all right? What should I do, I hope Meera is all right? By this time, I was sweating profusely. I was scared. My heart was thumping so loudly I thought I might have a heart attack any moment. My breathing was ragged and I could hear myself talking disjointedly. My brain was frozen, unable to send any signal of value. I was paralysed with fear.

I banged the door in despair with both my hands and then again turned the knob as an afterthought. I did not expect anything to happen and tried the knob more out of frustration that anything else. It swung open easily and I stared for a moment in complete bafflement. Had it been open all along? Had I made a terrible mistake? Could I have put Meera's life in jeopardy through my stupidity?

Meera was seated on the bathroom counter. She looked well and I burst out in relief. "Meera, why haven't you been answering me? Why didn't you open the door? Was it open all the time or did you just open it? I have been calling out for you. Are you all right? Why didn't you answer when I called you? I have been so worried about you imagining … imagining … anyway the main thing is that you are fine. You are fine aren't you?

She smiled at me. It was a strange smile, a very strange smile. Her eyes shone brightly like a thousand watt bulb and the centre appeared darker almost black in colour. Her lips were stretched wide from side to side but I did not see her teeth. It was a smile of appearance and did not look genuine. I felt a sense of disquiet engulf me.

I went up close to my wife and hugged her sitting form tightly. I stood clasping her to me with great relief. "Oh my dear Meera, my dearest sweet Meera. How worried I was. You can not imagine what has been going through my mind. But I see you are fine. And that is all that matters. I am so happy to see that you are all right. I am so happy ... so happy." She didn't move nor did she respond to my endearments and I stepped back uncertainly.

What was happening here ... what was the matter with Meera? Just that morning I had left behind a vibrant woman who had held me in her arms and had done things to my body that had made me write in ecstasy. She had launched an attack on my defenceless torso, ferreting out both the old and new tender spots of experimenting with great elan and gusto. I had no inhibitions in the face of such ingenuity and she had no limitations, no parameters to keep to. I let myself drift ... drift as she worked me into a frenzy. From serene lassitude to slow awakening and then tumultuous rapture – she certainly knew how to elicit the right response from me!

We enjoyed each other's bodies and our lovemaking was always innovative as well as unexpected. Being small and agile, Meera could assume the most outlandish of positions and thus our lovemaking tended to be somewhat acrobatic in nature. On the floor, on the edge of a chair, the table, even on the steps and the kitchen – nothing was left to the imagination. Every position was tried and the right ones were further experimented with, while the unimprovisable were discarded.

Having allowed Meera the initial initiative, I then took over. It was now my turn to please her already quivering body. I sought out her pleasure spots and worked on them with great fervour. She responded to my sexual expertise with delightful exhibitionism. Neither of us could stay in one position for long and after a few moments, we were once again on an acrobatic sojourn. After much tomfoolery and growing passion, we succumbed to the inevitable. With immense pleasure, we had come together. Sweat glistening on our bodies, sheets in disarray and furniture strewn all over the place, we contemplated each other in the aftermath of our volcanic lovemaking. Then with heightened senses and hearty appetites, we had eaten a wonderful breakfast that was interspersed with much laughter, early morning banter and sharing of food.

That was this morning ... not days ago, not weeks ago ... not some figment of my imagination. Who then, I asked myself, was this person?

Her eyes looked like bulging probes that held unfathomable secrets. They were dark and luminous. Her pointed little head appeared smaller and the close cropped hairstyle which I had never really taken to, seemed to accentuate her tiny ears. She licked her lips several times and her tongue darted in and out with a rapidity that had me mesmerized. It remined me of something ... of something ... but I couldn't place it at that moment. She was perched on the edge of the counter seemingly relaxed but somehow, I got the impression that she was poised on edge ... waiting ... waiting for something. One false move and ... and ... I didn't really know what could happen.

At that moment I could not fathom her mood, I failed to comprehend what had happened. My tired and muddled brain recognized that my wife was fine and for that moment it was enough, I needed to sleep, to rest my weary brain. "I'm going to bed. Come soon."

There was no response. I looked at her again. Her legs were crossed, one on top of the other, but so without flesh were her bony calves that they almost looked like one. Her little feet with their curved instep were pointed inwards. At this highly charged moment, I could be forgiven for thinking it looked very much ... like a tail.

I felt ill at the thought. A tail? What was wrong with me? Why was I thinking this way? I blamed it on my over active imagination coupled with my tiredness and the highly charged events that had just taken place. I looked at Meera whose gaze had not wavered from mine but bored into my skull like a red hot electric current. It was almost as if she could read my thoughts. I stepped back uncomfortably as she had just watched me silently. Why didn't she say anything?

As I walked out of the bathroom and closed the door for some unaccountable reason, I remembered the lizard I had seen scuttling across the ceiling in the morning.

# 2

# Flower

Mr. Desai left home at five sharp wearing his Tuesday outfit which consisted of light green corduroy trousers, and a yellow and red checked long sleeved brushed cotton shirt. He also wore his favourite brown tie-up walking shoes that were sturdy and he considered dependable despite having been on numerous visits to the shoemaker who knew every stitch in its leathery make-up as did the owner. He also took his walking stick bought many years ago on an office trip to Simla.

He looked sprightly and extremely fit for his seventy-two years and he took immense pride in his upright figure and the fact that he could still outwalk many a youngster. He walked through the market place with its half cobbled stone pathway and remnants of a new age tar road. The place was gloriously alive!

There were fruit vendors shouting out the prices of the luscious ruby red watermelon, sea green canteloupe and bright flame coloured oranges that smelt as sweet and as inviting as they looked. There were shoe polishers rubbing their brushes against their hands and coaxing passers-by to indulge their shoes. Tea stalls and sweet shops with huge cauldrons brimming with fat and luscious looking sweetmeats captivated the eye and sent aroma-filled signals to hungry customers. Bicycles, scooters and playing children shared the road with betel-chewing adults and cows ambled by as if they owned the place.

Mr. Desai negotiated each turn with great skill and precision. Ever so often he waved to a familiar face, stopped and chatted with a friendly acquaintenance, bought some supari, had a look at the magazine stall or simply walked along with great purpose.

The entire evening, from getting ready for the walk to the actual event itself was so ingrained in his mind, so much a part of him that he could have done it with his eyes closed. The path was a familiar one, very much a part of his mind for over thirty years. It was part of the landscape that needed no second look.

His gait was slow and deliberate. Each step had already been seen through many, many years back. He knew exactly where each foot went. The hole in the roads, the tree at the corner, the stone well that had stood alone for all these years. The unkempt flower patch, the broken water pump that sat in solitary dignity, a testimony to another age, a product of another time. The coconut tree that stood tall and proud and magnificent in its beauty and now a good friend for several years. He had overseen its growth, initially as an onlooker and then as the days, months and years went by, he was like an anxious parent, noting with approval and pride each new shoot and experiencing pangs of anxiety when a leaf turned too brown under the hot summer or the heavy rains left it looking spent and exhausted.

The unswerving, completely one dimensional outlook had been ingrained for too many years. It was not unlike the creases that take time to settle around the midriff. Initially there is some resistance but after a while it is easier to let them settle to a life of permanence than one of constant battle and one learns to console oneself in a number of ways. For instance, what was downright intolerable and ugly becomes moderately, unattractive and then eventually a part of the landscape. So the creases find their own happy medium and then they have found a home for good!

He hadn't always been like this. He had started out life full of vision, full of dreams and hopes that he was going to be different. He believed he was a romantic, he had done things in his life which he thought were romantic. But the very pressure of living, of work, of life had bogged him down. He had fought against it but eventually the onslaught had been too much and he had immersed himself in work. And so there was work and more work and more work. He had allowed himself to become mechanical. All that vision and romanticism had slowly been squeezed out of him like a lemon parts with its juice, without his realizing that he was offering no resistance. He was now dry and hard, the rind was all that remained of a once soft and luscious centre.

Once in a while the thought came to him with some regret that life was going by too fast, that it had all become too mundane, that he never seemed to have time for anything but his work as he moved up the corporate ladder. He worked very late hours and after that there was the socializing that had to be done. Not so much to relax and enjoy oneself but as a follow up to what went on during the day. So the cringing and the servile attitude still had to be kept intact. The only relief was that the drinks flowed freely and there was a lot to eat.

When the thought came to him, as it often did in those early years, that he had no life except his work, he pushed it aside, squashed it to a pulp insisting with his wife and his inner self that it would all eventually happen, it would all happen in good time. He just had to make a little more money, he just had to have one more meeting, he just had to make one more telephone call, he just had to do this, he just had to do that. He just had to … he just had to … he just had to. There were always excuses for work and none for anything else that was not associated with work. Yes, they could go to the latest movie if so and so from his office could also go. It was good for his work. The new restaurant that had just opened? By all means but with a whole group of other associates. A trip down South, Absolutely. It was where the company wanted to open its next office. A perfect opportunity to explore that possibility!

Work did not allow for any extra curricular activities that were not in some remote way work related. Soon the anguished pleas, the tearful looks, the pained experiences and the meaningful silences lessened in frequency till it settled down to a boring pattern that was day-to-day living.

What happened that day? Well, it had started out like any other day. He had risen at the crack of dawn and read the newspapers while sipping his cup of tea. Mrs. Desai had also been there and they had discussed the news with alacrity. Breakfast had been a slightly elaborate affair as they had a guest from out of town. It had been almost eleven o'clock before they had left the table. After seeing their friend off, Mr. Desai had gone to his study to make some calls and deal with pending issues like electricity and gas bills that needed to be paid. Mrs. Desai was going out for the day and would have lunch with some friends.

After a light lunch of sambar and dosa, made by their excellent cook, Ramu, Mr. Desai went off to have his afternoon nap. When he awoke next his wife was still not back and he prepared to go for his evening walk.

Mr. Desai was walking along as usual, doing all the things that came naturally to him, a force of habit. He spoke to the local butcher about the deteriorating quality of meat which was being sold in the marked and discussed the worsening conditions of the abbatoirs and hence the double cruelty being inflicted upon the animals. First their lives were going to be snuffed out and then they were not even allowed to live their last days in some kind of sanitary surroundings which would benefit both man and animal.

He even propounded the wisom of becoming a vegetarian to a bemused butcher who never managed to get in more than a few words and spent most of the time simply nodding his head in agreement.

He then yelled out a responsive greeting to the magazine vendor and again complained about the recent hike in this newspaper price and the corresponding down slide in the quality of writing. He stopped at the paan stall and bought his regular supari packet and then walked towards the palm tree. He opened the packet of supari and noticed the slight willowing of one of the branches of the tree. He went up close and touched it tenderly though examining it thoroughly to make sure it was not going to die but was just the neglect of the local gardener. He looked around for him and espied him in the distance. As he walked around the park, he couldn't help but admire the flowers.

It was winter time. A time of abundance. The local gardener had worked hard all year round to come up with something beautiful. The gladioli, dahlias, chrysanthemums and sunflowers all beckoned invitingly. Even a few tulips had taken root. The petunias and the hibiscus, the lilies – all individually beautiful, together made a grand picture. He stood for a moment taking in the beauty and wondered how quickly life had flown by.

Abruptly he decided to head home. He walked passed the gardener and simply nodded without stopping. The gardener seemed surprised he was so sure he was going to get a yelling about the dry leaf, but then one could always expect the unexpected from this sahib.

He moved quickly, stumbling now and again in his haste. He reached the end of the road and took a right turn into the colony. The house was at the end of the road. He passed the local flower seller as he did every day again noticing the glorious profusion of winter colours. Blood red gladioli, white and pink chrysanthemums, dahlias of an unbelievable size, orchids and soft peach dutch roses. His gaze took in the rich scene without stopping for even a moment. He came closer, closer and passed the vendor. He walked a few more steps and stopped straight in his tracks. He paused for a long moment in indecision and then turned around slowly.

A very unusual thought had taken him completely by surprise. Mrs. Desai loved flowers, perhaps today he could take her some. He stared at the peonies. A moment of indecision kept him rooted to the spot. Should he? He could not remember when he had last given her flowers. In fact, if he really thought about it, in all probability at least some thirty years had elapsed since he had last done that. She would be surprised. He turned around and walked very slowly towards the vendor. It was a short distance but his steps were slow, very very slow. The vendor looked at him askance. He was as surprised as Mr. Desai and more than a little taken aback. This sahib was part of the landscape did not suddenly change like this!

"Namaste sahib. Is everything all right?" he enquired. He didn't offer him any flowers. Years at the same corner had taught him that this was one sahib who didn't buy and the initial entreaties had soon given way to resignation and eventually a daily respectful salute.

When he said nothing but just stared at the flowers as if mesmerized, the vendor got worried. "Are you all right?" He looked at him closely. He certainly did appear strange. There was a growing air of urgency about him, a kind of suppressed excitement that was at complete variance with his cool and detached manner.

He then spoke slowly. "I want two, no, no, three … four, actually make it a dozen of those dahlias. Those will look good won't they? And add some baby's breath and some of those peach dutch roses. Should it be write or peach, eh? Well, what do you think?"

The vendor stared at him askance. "Well, well are you

going to take all day?" said Mr. Desai. "Are you going to give me the flowers or not?"

The vendor snapped out of his stupor. The sahib wanted the flowers and he needed to make a sale. He bent quickly to do his bidding hoping the very predictable sahib would not suddenly change his mind and he find himself out of a sale.

"Beautiful, they look absolutely beautiful," cooed the sahib his eyes opening and shutting like a camera shutter. At that moment the very staid Mr. Desai looking nothing like his former self. He was rocking backwards and forwards on his heels like an old rocking chair caught in suspended frenzy, his fingers were clasped tightly together and if anyone had cared to notice they were white, so tightly were they entwined in each other. His face had begun to glisten with tiny beads of perspiration and the back of his hair was damp and the tendrils all bunched together. He would not however have been amused to be likened to a fellow from a comic strip!

He took the flowers from the vendor, leaving him with a very handsome tip that restored him in the vendor's eyes as a possible customer.

He dashed off so fast he left a cloud of dust behind. He was half running and half trotting. His coordination seemed to have deserted him and he looked like an old mare struggling valiantly with a glorious past but now aged and mellow, wants to have one more tryst with past splendour.

He blazed into the house like a hurricane, sweat dripping from every pore, eyes wide and excited with a light that had almost disappeared over the yeas. In one hand he clutched the flowers, in the other his cane. He however, threw it on the living room sofa and held on to the balustrade as he made his way upstairs. By the time he reached the top of the landing he was out of breath. He was aroused and every vein in his body twitched in response to his nervous energy. Each step was too slow even though he had never walked so fast in all his life.

"Seema, Seema, where are you?" There was no response and he shouted out her name even louder. He went into their bedroom. It was empty. He looked around. The four poster antique bed had pride of place. Seema had found it in one of the back alleys of the old city and after much painstaking labour had brought out its inherent elegance and dignity. The intricate woodwork gleamed with years of caring.

The light silk rugs strewn all over the room were set to advantage against the fully upholstered two-seater cream sofa. It was extremely comfortable with the kind of cushions you could sink into. Against it was the foot rest that Seema knew he enjoyed using after a hard day at the office. There were paintings on the wall that he knew nothing about but which he had come to appreciate more for their increasing value. The paintings were mostly soft lines and muted colours but on closer study each painting had a strength that could not be overlooked. The light from the stone finished lamps provided a soft glow to the room. He paused for a moment appreciating the quiet beauty of the room.

He turned to leave the room to look for her elsewhere in the house, when from the corner of his eye he saw her sitting with her back to him in her favourite chair, a knotted cane and teak wood creation with soft melting purple cushions. She was up against the window looking onto the garden she had so lovingly created.

It was a smallish garden but appeared much larger through careful planting. The flowers had been grown at different heights. For instance the smaller ones such as sweetpea and azaleas were right up in front. Then the sunflowers, gladioli and dahlias, the larger flowers, were next. The much larger green bushes; the perennials came last along with the roses.

There were strategically placed stones and a small pond that gave it an extremely cooling ambience. It was Seema's little baby and frequently he would come home late to find her in the garden sitting on the wrought iron swing amidst the sweet smelling jasmine and jacaranda trees.

"Seema, why didn't you answer me? Anyway look what I have got for you."

He moved to the front of her and presented her with the flowers. He stared into her gentle face with its age-old lines. He stared at her red bindi, the soft white folds of her hair and the calm peaceful repose. He stared at the half smile that lingered, the contentment that lit up her face. He then stared at the flowers. Beautiful and vibrant in all their glory. But late, so very, very late.

# 3

# The Wives

Mehr heard the news just as she was lifting the boiling milk from the stove and pouring it into the pyrex dish to cool. Some of the milk splashed on her arm and scalded her. At once her skin became red and within minutes it looked sore and angry. From past experience she knew it was going to be with her for quite some time and would in all probability leave a mark. But it was not the hot searing pain that went to her heart. It was the news. It pierced right through her, with a suddenness that left her stunned. It tore her insides, devoured her reason and ravaged her emotions. She could feel the blood rise within her like molting lava and her heart felt like a thousand firecrackers going off at the same time.

She has put her hand to her heart in an attempt to calm herself but already the thoughts were crowding her mind and arising as fast as she put the previous one down. Could it be true? Would he betray her like this? The thought was unbearable. No, no it was not possible. He was just not that type of man, that kind of human being. He knew how much she loved him and he would never insult her in this manner. For that is what it amounted to An insult.

She looked at her neighbour's face, inquisitive and watchful. The eyes were narrowed and there was an obvious air of wicked glee and anticipation. Mehr could see Anita noting her every move and hoping there was a story to tell the other womenfolk when she returned. Of course, she would embellish the account with all kinds of details that had never actually taken place! "God, please don't let it be true, please don't let it be true," she whispered silently to herself. She resolutely straightened her back and held her head high. There was no way she was going to give the old cow the satisfaction of seeing her break down. She had to keep her pride and dignity intact.

"Anita, you could not have heard correctly. Now please let me get on with my chores. I have so much to do and I know you have a lot to do too." Anita thwarted of her desire to glean some scandalous tidbit gave a loud grunt with disappointment writ large on her face. But she did not leave without a parting bombshell. "You might not believe it but it is true. And from all accounts the new wife is both young and beautiful."

Mehr sank to the floor once Anita had left the house and sobbed piteously. So it had finally happened. All these years of seeing other wives have their dignity stripped. Of seeing their hearts broken and their happiness destroyed. Their smiling content faces changing to fear and resentment and eventual subjugation. All these years she had stood apart and now it had happened to her too. The inevitable had happened. Shekhar had taken a second wife.

Having cried her heart out, she brushed her tears aside and tried to do the same with her fears. Why was she crying like this. The news might not be true. After all they had been married for so many years now and Shekhar had not given the slightest indication that he was unhappy with her or had any reason to look for another wife. With that thought in her mind, she resolutely set aside her fears and went about preparing the evening meal.

Mehr had always been the centre of attention. With four adoring brothers and indulging parents catering to her every desire, friends and admirers who were fascinated by her vivacious personality and generous nature, she was the focus of attention wherever she went. She was the pride of the whole family. And everyone agreed that she was indeed blessed.

Mehr was a beautiful woman with all the requisite attributes that were considered necessary to distinguish her from the average. She was tall and slim with curves in all the right places and was extremely fair with features that invariably made one gasp. Long dark eyebrows under which were huge light green eyes, a strong patrician nose and full ruby red lips that often needed no artifice. Her hair was jet black and flowed in sinuous abandon till her waist. She had never given in to fashion and it stood out all the more in an age of short and trim.

Apart from an astonishing physical beauty, Mehr was endowed with a keen and inquiring mind, a natural intelligence that went beyond the average. She was a formidable adversary and loyal friend and had admirers in droves ever since her thirteenth birthday when her figure began to take shape and its voluptuousness could no longer be concealed.

She was naturally not unaware of her charms and a certain confidence became an inbuilt attribute. Thus when she eventually married, she chose from the cream of the crop and knew with an innate certainty that she was likewise the pick for him.

She had got married at the reasonable age of twenty-three, her parents believing that education was important and while a career was not essential, a sound education provided an important grounding and was there to fall back upon in times of need should it ever arise. Thus, she was one of those wives any husband could be proud of and she believed her husband appreciated her and understood her worth.

Although she loved her husband dearly, she was not

'in' love with him. He had failed to kindle the depths of her passion or to plummet that indefinable emotion. Mehr believed the actual physicality of the act, touching or kissing the other person was naturally pleasurable, but in a sense it was only a first step. And as one became more involved in the act, one transcended that state of emotion and reached a level of greater consciousness.

Mehr had never experienced such a feeling though she firmly believed it existed. Thus, now and then, she felt a restlessness, an inner voice that continually questioned her need for something ... more fulfilling. While the act itself took place on a fairly regular basis, she did not feel sexually fulfilled.

There was no excitement and she no longer felt any deep pleasure. Sex had become boring and repetitive. Shekhar stuck to set a pattern that left no room for the imagination. There were no hidden contours and unknown erogenous areas to explore. But Mehr could be wild and aggressive in the bedroom, possessing a latent wanton, even lascivious side that needed to be released and further examined.

Unfortunately, Shekhar was blind to her sexual desires. Thus, she fulfilled her own need for the unusual through her fevered imagination. She had erotic fantasies her husband knew nothing about and if he had, he would probably have been shocked. Tied to the bed, whipped to submission, out in a public area – these were all yearnings that needed to be explored. But excitement of this nature was a distant dream for Mehr. Sex was always predictable and Shekhar was always supposed to be the initiator. Of course, she did at times take the lead but then he could never just lie back and enjoy himself. He always felt he had to be in control, the master. To just lie back felt a lot like submission.

So, he would nuzzle her breasts and bite the nipples. She hated him doing so and despite her repeated protests, he continued as if he did not believe her. She had never been able to understand why he did that. Was it a force of habit that precluded anything different because it meant entering unknown terrain or was it simply a chauvinistic attitude which adhered to the maxim that the man was the master and he always knew best?

He would push her head back and kiss her with urgency. But the urgency was always the same. It had a predictability that took away from its intentness. With no further titillation and now himself aroused he would enter her still dry inner self, satiation only a spasm away from completion.

Mehr's arousal was always slow, but once kindled, she could be fiery and aggressive. Shekhar, unfortunately had never seen this side of her. By the time she was aroused with the help of her own erotic fantasies and not Shekhar's inept and cursory licking and squeezing, he was already on the point of ejaculation. This always left her unsatisfied. Any attempt on her part to discuss their sexual incompatibility or incompleteness brought no response as if he didn't see it.

Sex for Shekhar was completely straightforward. He thought of himself as a good lover and would have been surprised if he had learnt how inept he was in Mehr's eyes. Although he did have naughty and lewd thoughts like any other man, there was a point beyond which he would not go. Hence, looking at magazines and pornographic films was fine, true it was voyeuristic but since it stimulated the sexual juices in a harmless manner it could be indulged. But anything more creative, eccentric or unpredictable was viewed as deviant and kinky and an attempt into this realm was completely and utterly pariah.

Thus, Mehr had managed this far to ignore these rumblings and they had remained undetected by Shekhar. Other than this "painful void" as she saw it, she was relatively content and believed her marriage was in all other aspects an admirable. She had two children, a boy and a girl, a husband who was handsome as well as successful and most important, a good human being. Everything was going just fine.

Shekhar was a quiet sort of fellow. He appeared reserved and aloof to the world at large but with his wife and family it was a different matter. He was passionately devoted to them. He was kind and gentle and had some of the character that Mehr possessed though he lacked her strength and dept of imagination. He was quite an undemonstrative man in public but his devotion to his wife was, well, almost legendary.

Or so she thought.

Dusk fell and soon the house was bathed in the golden glow of the setting evening sun. The birds twittered as they flew back home, the sky had turned a beautiful purple and there was a slight breeze in the air that accentuated the sweet smell of frangipani and jasmine from the garden. She had bathed and was sitting on the terrace at ease with the beauty around her but uneasy in mind and spirit. Only she knew how tortuous the day had been. The turmoil inside her was painful and gripping. It had invaded her entrails and had lodged itself with a permanence that was frighteningly prophetic.

She prayed that the news was not true but the disquietening feeling and sense of dread that had stayed with her all day told another story. Its ominous presence was a dark cloud that grew in intensity as evening approached and now it was a raging catalyst waiting to erupt.

He walked into the house long after the light had faded. The small insects hovered by the candlelight dancing in the warm glow. Now and then the zing of their bodies sizzling could be heard as they moved to near the flame. She had watched as they danced the dance of death, they were doomed from the very first moment they saw the light. They seemed to know the inherent dangers and yet were mesmerized.

There was no shame on his face, no guilt whatsoever. He walked into the house, or at least attempted to with the same heartiness that he commanded every day. But she knew. The very moment she saw his face she knew. She had awaited his arrival with hope and dread but any flickering hope that the news was not true vanished the moment she looked into his eyes. Oh those eyes! She had looked into them a thousand times and seen her image always. But the large light hazel eyes were clouded and try as she might there was no picture of her there.

He knew he had wounded her deeply, worse had had humiliated her. She was a strong woman, proud and dignified and could withstand almost anything. But this was altogether different. He had behaved badly, gone against the grain and he knew the sense of shame and the pain his action had caused. Her pride had been wounded and for that she would not forgive him easily.

At that moment she just wanted to die. As she stared at him she wondered how she was going to ever be able to live with the numbing pain that had lodged itself in her heart. She knew it sounded melodramatic but she didn't mean it to be. Die for a man who had treated her so shabbily! Now she finally understood all those women before her, ahh!...yeh!...what agony. To be treated so shabbily, to be stabbed in the back by the person you least expect. Death at this moment would be so blissful. It would mean an end to this suffering and shame.

Shekhar avoided looking at her directly. It was unthinkable! This man who used to stare straight into her eyes was now shuffling about like some village idiot!

"So you heard?"

"Did you think I wouldn't?" she replied caustically. His face turned a dull red and it made her even angrier. How dare he? How dare he walk in with that stupid look on his face and expect her to behave in the same manner as if his action had no consequence whatsoever? How dare he?

"Now, now Mehr. I was going to tell you before I decided. But it all happened so quickly."

"Are you telling me you have just met her and like a fool married her without thinking about the consequences because your over active libido had taken control from your brains or are you saying ... do you have the gall to tell me you have been carrying on with this ... this woman, behind my back all the while acting as if nothing was wrong? Have you been betraying me ... me ... my love and trust for you and living a lie all this time?"

She knew she was screaming and shouting like a fish wife, like all those other women she had seen betrayed and demoralized. She despised what she was doing, what she was becoming but the pain egged her on and she couldn't help herself. She cried copiously as if her heart was breaking.

The day passed. Life had to go on and she had to accept the inevitable. The second wife was a silly young thing called Nilima. Her characteristic trademark was her constant girlish giggling that could be set off at the slightest provocation. How she hated that sound! It soon became apparent that she was vain and empty headed, a disastrous combination to witness as an outsider but pure hell when living with someone at close quarters.

After a while, as she had hoped, Shekhar began to lose interest. He was an intelligent man and while initially besotted, he could not countenance stupidity for long. Nilima's daily beauty regime took the whole morning, after which she would have a long siesta in the afternoon to recover from the strenuous ablutions she had performed. The evening was set aside to decide what clothes to wear and new hairstyle to try, along with some other scatter-brained girls from the locality who seemed to always hang around the house. By the time Shekhar came home, tired and often absorbed in his work, all he saw was this painted doll who looked good and needed to be admired and pampered. At first it had felt good to look upon this work of art and it flattered his ego to think that she did it all for him. But the novelty soon wore off.

She did not want to hear about his day at work or discuss events both local and international. Oh no. She just wanted a slave to pander to him whims. Her dressing up, he soon realized, was not so much for him as for herself. She wanted him take her out every evening where she could be further admired and where others could listen to her silly talk.

For a while, Shekhar indulged her as he would a pretty child. He came home early from work just to be with her and every night was party night. A lot of time was spent in the bedroom and with all the sounds emanating from there, Mehr wondered if he had become more innovative though she doubted it. He listened to her foolish talk and even started to respond in that older way that sugar daddies do; smiling for no reason, having no secret code of talking and letting her get away with murder even though he looked like a fool and probably knew it too.

However, it soon became evident that he was no longer enamoured of the flutter of her eyelashes that had so captivated him in the beginning or her long nails that she painted red and had in the past sent him wild with desire when she lightly ran them up his thigh. Her set patterns had begun to grate on his nerves and after only one year of marriage, he preferred the company of his first wife.

Nilima saw the transformation taking place from besotted, cuckolded lover to irritated suitor and eventually disgruntled husband. All these changes had no initial impact on her. She went blithely along with her life, refusing to let the world at large and her husband's increasing moodiness disturb her.

Being straightforward and devoid of guile or harbouring any resentment, Mehr tried to reason with her. But to no avail. She was extremely spoilt and could still not see the wisdom of changing herself.

Slowly, Shekhar took to spending more and more time with Mehr. He started with little excuses, "there's no hot water in the bathroom" or "have you got anything to eat, she's not feeling well enough to cook." Soon the subterfuge was dropped; "she's giving me a headache with her stupid talk". "Can you believe she didn't know the elections were going on in the country?" and eventually "she's driving me crazy, I don't know why I married her."

All this while Mehr made sympathetic noises but to be fair she defended the girl. "You knew all this when you married her. She is still the same girl and you have no right to complain about her to me. No right at all." He was surprised at her attitude, expecting perhaps a sympathetic ear and mentioned this to her.

He knew Mehr's strength of character and her definite beliefs in what was right or wrong. But this was really too much!

"I don't understand you. Here I am, having done you a grave injustice and instead of taking my side against this woman, you defend her as if she had been wronged."

"Well," she resorted, "the blame lies with you. You should have known better than to marry someone half your age but now that you have, you jolly well stick by it. You men," she said scathingly, "are all alike. You think women have no feelings and can be treated accordingly. One day its one woman and the next day, if the fancy takes you, its another. Well not here, definitely here. Do not treat women so shabbily. Besides, Nimila has my sympathy for marrying you. She needs it more than you do!" At that he would laugh loudly and the conversation would invariably take another turn.

Soon after that Shekhar left on a business trip which would keep him away for a few months and the two wives were left to look after each other. Mehr being the older of the two was immediately cast in the role of listener, while the second wife spent all her time complaining about how 'he' has changed. The two being thrown together for days on end became close in that disparate way that two strangers, with very little in common, become, when left on their own. Both knew that once the situation reverted to normal, they would again assume their previous roles.

The two women shared the same room at night after it became apparent that Nilima was afraid of the dark without her 'husband' by her side and Mehr felt that if she was going to get any sleep they had better join forces for a while. It was better than hearing her scream and listening to her turn the lights on and off at three second intervals. She had no wish for this kind of nightlife and common sense made her acquiesce.

It was a strange time. Two wives thrown together with absolutely nothing in common except their husband. But they managed quite well. At night they would talk about their lives before marriage, their dreams, their disappointments, life at present, their identity as women and the callous attitude of men towards them. They slowly opened up to each other and in doing so learnt about each other's foibles. They also developed a genuine liking for each other!

Shekhar arrived after a few months. The business trip had gone well and he was in an expansive frame of mind. He had plenty of time to think about what he had done. He had decided to send his second wife back to her parents, though magnanimously not divorcing her "keeping her reputation in mind."

The following morning after his return, the entire neighbourhood woke up to their fighting. It was an argument between the three of them. Although the voices were muffled there was much throwing of furniture and breaking of glass.

As the fight gained in intensity, the entire neighbourhood gathered outside the house to see what would happen. Which of the wives was being given the boot? As time went by, people started betting, the neighbourhood chaat wallah moved his stall and did a roaring business while chairs and rope beds were brought to sit down upon.

Eventually the main door opened. The chorus of voices stopped abruptly, everyone waited with bated breath … who would it be … who was going away … Mehr or Nilima?

As the door opened wider, the crowd gave a united gasp. It couldn't be. Out stepped Shekhar, a scowl on his face and luggage in hand. As he walked away the two wives smiled at each other and went inside closing the door behind them!

# 4

# The Hotel : An Episode

The black and yellow dilapidated taxi came to a halt with a screech that threw us both forward. Our hands went out in front to support us and we found ourselves squashed against the front seat of the car. It was not the entry I had envisaged and I at once felt my confidence ebb and my dignified mien crumble slightly. I got out immediately cursing the driver, though quietly, under my breath for fear of drawing attention to ourselves. But Masi refused to step out.

"The doorman is supposed to open the door," she whispered "why isn't he coming?"

Almost as if everyone else had heard her they turned round to see what was happening including the doorman of the imposing hotel. "Masi please," I implored beseechingly. "Get out of the taxi. Everyone is looking."

Although people had stopped looking at us the doorman still continued to stare down the breadth of his huge nose without any attempt at pretence, all the while making it very obvious that he was certainly not going to open the hotel's equally imposing doors – as they did in all the movies. Certainly not the door of a mere taxi. Especially when there were so many Mercedes and BMWs to choose from.

When then it never ever happens like it does in the movies. While I was going hot and cold and cursing the wretched man for making me feel so small, so inadequate and out of depth, one thought kept running through my head was how easy it was to demoralize people and especially people like us. Another part of me was thinking that the scenario would have been quite different if we had been someone of importance then he would no doubt have been fawning all over us.

Why were we so overlookable? Perhaps it was Masi's bold orange sari with green flowers that were altogether too loud and so obviously of the cheapest cotton or perhaps it was the peaceful nondescript face that had never been enslaved by artifice and thus merged serenely with the crowds. Or maybe it was me, my usually oiled plaits were left open almost touching my waist. Maybe it was the two-year-old ghagra from the Handloom Emporium that had seen better days and was an attempt on my part to appear modern (a big change from the traditional salwar kurta I was regularly seen in). Then looking at my non-varnished toes in sensible though hardly exciting kolapuri chappals, I wondered if perhaps that was it!

Masi eventually realized that the doorman was not going to open her door and got out ungainly mumbling under her breath. We walked up the stairs and Masi stumbled slightly. I caught the doorman's sneer through the corner of my eye and mentally socked him while hurrying her on. My attempts to appear cool and collected were thwarted in that instant and my immediate thought was to flee from the scene. But there was no going back. Masi was extremely excited. Her eyes were wide as saucers. She clasped my hand tightly and sucked her breath in at the wondrous sight they met her. As we entered the hotel lobby it seemed all eyes were upon us, Masi in her too, too loud sari and me in my (till that moment) chic ghagra.

We walked through the huge lobby trying not to gape at everything – the huge chandeliers, the imposing paintings, the plush carpets, the indefinable air of grooming and polish. We were engulfed in another world so different from our own, we could hardly breathe. We entered the coffee shop with relief and I immediately espied a vacant table. We moved towards it with the speed of lightning but were caught midway.

"Yes, can I help you?" said the steward with a bored look on his face and a tone that should have been several shades sweeter.

"Can we have a table for two please?" the words were barely out before the steward had disappeared towards a vision in pearls and smoky chiffon while we looked on in awe. The fawning was false and contrived and continued for what seemed an interminable time while we stood around helplessly. Eventually Masi decided to assert herself. She raised her voice a decibel; "escuse please, please escuse, table for us two" she gesticulated. But no one was listening and I could have died of embarrassment as people turned and stared. They looked us up and down as if we were dirt and I realized what the saying `to crawl under something and hide' truly meant for at that moment I would have given anything to be somewhere else.

This wasn't our place. We didn't belong here. And it was bad enough that we knew it, what made it worse was others seemed to know it too. But there was nothing I could do. Masi had insisted we go to a Five 'ishtar' hotel to celebrate the passing of my final B.A. exams. She had been saving for months and I too, had been waiting anxiously for the day when we would go. All my friends knew about the outing and I was sure the whole locality did too. It was something I hadn't exactly kept to myself. And so here we were. What an absolute fool I had been. I should have realized what I was letting myself in for. I could not stop berating myself. God, what a fool. A stupid, stupid fool. I was raging inside unable to decide what to do. I felt like leaving straightaway and even whispered urgently to Masi, "let's leave and go some place else" but she would not hear of it. "I've waited for a long time to come here and we are certainly not leaving without having something to eat." With Masi in this mood there was no arguing. And that was that.

Needless to say 'our table' had long been filled. We waited for the next table – two unimportant people striving to appear nonchalant in a world of glitter and pomp. Finally, we got a table in the very centre of the room which would have pleased me no end not so long ago but now I would have gladly settled for obscurity. Something in the corner where we wouldn't be noticed. But it wasn't to be. The steward was none too pleased at giving us such a prominent table, in fact one of the best, but nothing else was available and he knew he could not make us wait any longer.

For a few minutes we were both silent. We looked in awe at our surroundings. Everywhere people were talking and laughing. They seemed to be everything we were not. Clearly sophisticated, others were noisy and loud. They had an air about them ... of total ease, obviously eating in a coffee shop was no big deal and did not evince the kind of calamitous state we found ourselves in.

The salad bar in the middle of the room was almost hypnotic. Try as much as I could to prevent it, my eyes kept straying towards the food and I could see Masi lick her lips in anticipation. The table was simply laden with every possible food. We had never seen anything like it in our lives except in the movies and our eyes nearly bulged at the gargantuan mounds. There was every kind of temptation displayed to full effect. I counted ten different salads in varying colours, an array of meats of which I am sure I wouldn't have known the names even if I tried and desserts, that made me want to jump for joy. They were there in every conceivable shape and size. The strawberry tart looked scrumptious and beside it the profiteroles that I could now recognize (I had spent an hour in the local bookshop looking at cookery books to make sure I knew what was what) seemed perfectly rounded, oozing with cream and a thick chocolaty sauce, just the way they were meant to be.

The tempting array had whetted my appetite and I could see that Masi felt the same way. I leaned towards her and said quietly, "looks really good doesn't it? I'm thinking of trying the strawberry tart.'

Masi smiled at my barely concealed excitement and nodded towards the profiteroles. "I didn't know what those round chocolate things are but they look delicious. What about trying them?"

Just then the waiter arrived with the menus and my excitement evaporated instantly. I closed my eyes in dismay. This couldn't be. It wasn't true. Cold coffee for Rs.80 and a plate of pakoras for Rs.45! And added to that were the taxes. There was definitely no chance of having anything extravagant, the strawberry tart or the profiteroles once again seemed a remote dream. What was Masi thinking? I had never seen her with more than Rs.10. I broke out in a cold sweat. What if she didn't have enough money? God, that was all we needed. I had to ask.

"Masi! Masi ... do you have enough money?" I whispered with frantic anxiety. It was the wrong time to have done so and sheer bad luck because just at that very moment one of the waiters passed by and his smirk became all the more pronounced.

"Now worry shurry," said Masi gaily. "Just relax and enjoy yourself. I want this to be a memorable outing for you. You certainly deserve it" and she buried her nose in the menu once again.

I finally decided to have tea (which was the cheapest of the lot) and a piece of strawberry tart which Masi insisted upon while Masi decided to have "ishpresso' coffee with the complimentary biscuits from Italy which were part of a current promotion. We looked around for the waiter but no one ventured forth to our table despite several pleading looks from my side. Finally Masi told me to call out, "I don't think I should do that," I said "someone will come eventually."

After another five minutes when nobody showed up at our table, Masi again prodded me to call out. I looked around, wriggled in my seat and raised my hands but was ignored. Totally, I turned my head this way and that, hoping to catch their eye, but to no avail. Finally embarrassed to death but also angry, I yelled out loudly. I surprised myself. My voice did not come out in the squeak I half expected but loud and clear and ringing with authority. I didn't have to wait for a second before a waiter hurried forward.

I placed the order in what I hoped was a confident tone (I had practised it enough times at home) but Masi spoiled it by pronouncing espresso as 'ishpresso' thrice despite my earlier tutoring at home.

The waiter smiled superciliously. "You mean an espresso coffee, don't you, Madam?" he asked Masi.

"Yes, yes," she replied happily, `ishpresso'.

"Anything else, Madam?" he asked. I felt my cheeks burn, for somehow he knew there wasn't. How I would have liked to throttle his neck or at least put him in his place by ordering the most extravagant item on the menu. But I knew it wasn't fair to Masi. And anyway he whisked off before I could put my plan into action – perhaps he had seen the mad gleam in my eye.

I looked around. People were talking, laughing even shouting. The place was crowded and everyone was having a good time. We were gobbling as much as we could with our eyes – the huge windows in the ceiling through which the sunlight came through, the white marble floor, the beautiful paintings that adorned each wall, the plants and gorgeous flower arrangement, orchids, gladioli, ponsettia, strewn all over and the clothes and jewellery flashing around us – we didn't need to ask each other but we both wondered what they cost and again I wondered what on earth were we doing here. While nobody bothered to even notice us for which I was thankful, when they did by pure accident perchance to glance our way it was with contempt, the look that said we were nobodies and nobodies were not supposed to be there.

Our order arrived after a long interval in which guests arriving after us were served. Before the waiter could place the cups down Masi pounced on him.

"Where are the complimentary biscuits?" she hissed.

"They are finished," he said and smiled with what seemed to me more than ordinary delight.

Masi looked crestfallen. "But, but she stuttered ... they are complimentary ... they cannot finish ... are you absolutely sure?" she added almost pleadingly.

I could not bear the sad look on Masi's face. "But you never said anything when we placed the order," I said defiantly.

The waiter looked bored. He spoke slowly and very deliberately, enunciating every word as you would a child or cretin. "As I just said they are finished, finished." And he joined his hands to add credence to what he was saying. Then more as a reflex than any real wish to help he added, "Is there anything else you would like to order?" "No," she mumbled almost sadly and he went away with what seemed an extra spring to his step. The tea was cold but I did not have the nerve to complain ... and even if I did they would probably come up with a good excuse. We both sat in silence sipping our drinks and deep in our own thoughts.

After a while, I noticed the waiter place a plate of

exquisitely turned out biscuits on an equally exquisite plate besides the espresso of a well turned out lady. Horror of horrors, they were the complimentary biscuits Masi had ordered. I turned to Masi hoping she hadn't seen but she was staring at them her mouth agape.

"It's the same biscuits I ordered," she said loudly.

I flinched with shame. "Don't shout," I told her in embarrassment.

"But that is my plate of biscuits," she wailed. "I asked for those biscuits first and the waiter said they were all finished. You heard him didn't you?" she looked at me for a moment and then turned away. "Liar ... liar ... liar ..." she shouted her voice getting louder and louder.

"Please Masi", I said flushing red with embarrassment and hoping no one had heard "just forget about it. There only biscuits, please, please." By now it seemed the whole coffee shop was staring at us and worse still, some people had started sniggering.

"Waiter," Masi shouted before I could stop her. When he just stared at us and continued in the other direction she shouted out even more loudly across the room, "waiter, my biscuits, I want my complimentary biscuits."

Suddenly I felt physically sick. The desire to faint was acute but I knew I couldn't add further to the disastrous situation. I wanted to get out of there, out of the stuck up rarefied air conditioned glitz that was alien to me as I was to it. What had ever possessed me to come here? I must have been made to ever agree. Yes definitely mad.

The waiter eventually came towards us. He knew the type of people he was dealing with; gauche, hesitant and awkward. Unused to Five Star culture where the golden rule of clients being akin to gods prevailed. But we didn't know this and he had recognized this fact and was making the most of it. It showed in his deliberate swagger and supercilious rise of the eyebrows.

"The Madam was here before you and got the last plate.

Kindly do not create a scene." Masi's face went red with embarrassment. She looked like she was going to cry. But by some miracle she managed to regain her composure and instead spoke quietly but with dignity.

"That is a lie," she said. "I came here first, I ordered first and I should get the plate first."

The waiter looked around him and shrugged his shoulders which seemed to infuriate Masi even further.

"I know its all about money," she said bitterly. "Well," and she smiled triumphantly. "I have the money. See, see," she said and out of her bosom, the repository of all that was cherished, came the rumpled hanky so much a part of the average Indian woman, and in which were neatly rolled Rs.ten notes.

A kind of nausea overtook me and my head swam. Why had we ever ventured on so reckless an adventure? What were we doing here? We were crazy to have come here in the first place. This was not our milieu. Masi couldn't have been thinking straight but nor was I. We didn't belong here and never would. I just wished the ground wound open up and swallow me.

"Masi please," I implored her, "please keep quiet. Calm down, can't you see you are making a scene? Please let us just go. Let us get out of here as quickly as possible. Anyway, I added, I am not enjoying myself and would like to leave."

She did not expect me to betray her so easily or give up for that matter and looked at me for a long moment in what seemed stunned surprise. Her look was reproachful as if to say; 'what, you too?' But just as suddenly as she had yelled she became quiet.

I asked for the bill with some trepidation predicting another senseless wait and it hurt to realize that the embarrassing speed with which it was presented meant that the hotel staff were as eager to see the last of us as we were to get out of the place. Masi refused to tip while counting and recounting her money with a slowness that grated on my already fraught nerves.

After what seemed like forever the bill was finally settled and we got up to leave. The relief on both sides was apparent and in any other context would have made me laugh but now it was all too sad and depressing.

We were both disillusioned. The early euphoria had long since vanished. Masi had a tired look on her face that seemed to be her trademark and had always been there as far back as I can remember. I now realized that her tired look had almost disappeared when we had embarked on our adventure and till we had arrived at our destination in had all but gone.

With as much dignity as we could muster, we walked out of the hotel. There was a sense of déjà vu as we left. Once again the doorman at the entrance did not deign to open the doors for us. Anyway he was too busy seeing off a high flying party to bother about two nondescript females who had come and gone with little fanfare.

We held on to each other tightly as we walked to the bottom of the hotel driveway where a group of three wheeler scooters were parked. We plunged into one with extravagant haste and for once Masi did not bother to haggle about the fare as was usually the case.

It was dark already and the temperature had cooled down. The sounds of chattering voices, fried food and much hooting filled the air. As the three wheeler sputtered and roared we settled ourselves comfortably. On the right of the scooter was a picture of the Goddess Sita with a tinsel garland hanging around it. To the left was a picture of the elegant God Ganesh smothered with flowers. The rest of the scooter was plastered with pictures of current film stars. Neither of us looked back and we smiled happily as we gave the order to take us home.

# 5

# Mitra's Breakfast

Mitra was barely awake when Sheila drew the curtains aside and let the sun blaze through. It lit up the whole room making wonderful dancing patterns on the walls and for a few moment she just stared at the enchanting picture. The incandescent glow was the reminder of a new day … the red bougainvillea growing in abundance, ablaze … a profusion of colour that could not be ignored, the cypress that remained evergreen … and the sky … the sky was a glorious blue … not a cumulus in sight. It tugged at the heart strings and made you want to rush outside and be thankful for being … yes, just being alive.

Caught up in the almost painful beauty of it all, it was a few moments before Mitra got a grip on her slumbering senses. And when she did it dawned on her that there was someone else in the room. Looking at the woman in front of her brought no gleam of recognition and she struggled to sit up when she realized that the woman was a complete stranger.

Mitra stared at the well turned out woman past her prime standing at the foot of the bed. There was an air of quiet dignity about her that was unmistakable. Her clothes had obviously seen better days. The sari had obviously once been fuchsia but was now an indescribable mishmash that could have been anything and the blouse, definitely belonged to something else. But at least, she thought, they were clean.

However it was not her clothes that drew one's attention, it was her eyes. They seemed to fill her whole face and detracted from the almost ugly features; the flat nose, thick lips, nondescript hair and ears that defied description. Yes, it was definitely the eyes that one succumbed to, they were vibrant and compellingly alive and filled with an obvious gentleness that would be impossible to resist.

After looking her up and down several times, Mitra asked her who she was with obvious puzzlement though with an imperiousness that bordered on the rude.

Sheila seemed to find the question amusing and laughed uproariously but there was every evidence of kindness in her laughter and she shook her head indulgently. "We are not playing that old game again are we?"

That was certainly not the response Mitra expected and she stared at her incredulously, her anger and indignation clearly visible. "What on earth are you talking about?"

She drew herself upright as far as it was possible while sitting in bed and said haughtily, "I have no idea who you are or where you have come from. I cannot imagine who could possibly have hired you. You are insolent and I will certainly not stand for it. So," she added with a tight smile, "if you do not correct yourself immediately, I can assure you, you will not be here for very much longer."

Sheila fairly groaned out loud and raised her hands up in the air. "All right, all right," she answered. "We will play it your way even though it does you no good. And you know that even if you do not want to acknowledge it."

"Just what are you talking about, eh, eh?", said Mitra ferociously. "This is no game. Why everyone knows that I am the reigning princess of Jodhapura. You are obviously new and uneducated, otherwise you would not dare talk to me the way you are doing so. And if you want to remain here you had better brush up your act or it will be curtains for you. You are both rude and insolent and I shall not tolerate such behaviour again."

They both stared at each other for a long moment. Mitra then continued arrogantly, "Well! well? What are you gawking at me for? Hurry up and get me my breakfast."

"But" … for a moment Sheila looked nonplussed and it seemed she wanted to say more but thought better of it.

"Yes, your highness," she said gently, all trace of laughter gone and with a little curtsy and quick backward glance, she hurried out of the bedroom.

Mitra lay down with a sigh and relaxed luxuriantly against the pillows piled high on her back. Now that I have settled that, what should I do today she mused. There were many many options to choose from and in her mind each one more exciting than the other.

Let's see, she mused. I could go and see Sanjiv at his newly constructed farmhouse, take a swim in his heart shaped pool where I can wear my deliciously daring new swimsuit which arrived from Paris yesterday. Then have lunch with him, alone of course, in cosy intimacy and later perhaps we could go for a ride or maybe … another thought came to mind … may be I had better go into town with Shabu and do some shopping. I desperately need some new clothes and I am way behind the other girls who would surely have picked up the latest new designs. Yes … yes! that sounds promising.

The thought brought an instant thrill of excitement that shot right through her body as she imagined herself walking into the snootiest shop in town and buying the most expensive and exclusive of items.

She could just picture the whole outing. The visit would go something like this.

"Madam," the owner would of course be tripping all over himself at the excitement of seeing her in his shop.

After all she was an esteemed customer in the `A' bracket.

"It is so good to see you, how very very kind of you to grace my modest shop, how can we be of service?"

But before even waiting for her answer, he would continue in the same breath all the while skipping around her like a perfect idiot.

"We have some beautiful saris, absolute beauties" and his already stretched face would further widen to an almost inimaginable degree.

"Masterpieces that arrived just this morning! They are of course original one off pieces and naturally of the finest quality, only for someone of your distinctive choice."

By now he would be so obviously out of breath having skipped himself into a frenzy, she would have to take pity on him and say; "Really?" in a bored tone betraying none of her inner excitement.

And that would be signal enough for him to show her the most expensive pieces he had. It was a game they all played and every time it was the same. Oh yes, she could just see it all. It would be such fun. Apart from the obvious flattery which she could never get enough of, just being with all those breathtakingly beautiful saris would be a treat. And in her mind she could almost see the glorious saris in a multitude of colours, each more exquisite than the other. Just thinking about it made her feel faint.

She sank further into the bed, stretching her legs ecstatically. After all that shopping she knew she was bound to feel hungry ... where should she go to eat..? 'The Express Tower' ... uh, well maybe ..." I know I've got it," she yelled out loud and snapped her fingers. What better place to go to than that exclusive new restaurant, 'The Rendezvous'. The only place in town that could still be called exclusive mainly because the prices were truly exorbitant. Then also, there were always reporters hanging around for a glimpse of the famous. She might even get her picture taken! Now that would be quite something!

She smiled to herself as she mulled over the various options and mentally saw herself in each scenario with flattering images of herself flashing through her mind. The image of being the cynosure of all in town pleased her the most.

Well, she thought it was decided – she would go into town. She could wear her new lime green Benarsi sari with the matching sandals and of course her favourite pearl earrings. But then again what about the cream and gold salwar kurta that had an extremely provocative deckle edged neck line and fitted her like a second skin?

Of course, she would have to take the maid with her as her chaperone. Unmarried girls from her type of family, no matter what age, were not allowed to roam the streets alone. It was not consider quite the done thing and her father would be terribly annoyed.

She paused for a moment in thought. Could she, dare she go alone? She felt a thrill of excitement but she immediately quashed the idea. No, it required too much effort and was not worth the risk at the moment. There was nothing she could do but take the maid. But she was not going to allow her to ruin her plans. The maid could quite easily be disposed of later when she met another friend. She could go to the Hilton coffee shop where she would bump into Hita and Natasha. She knew they lunched there every alternate day. But this would be done all very accidentally of course!

It was the perfect opportunity to show off her white and gold outfit (the lime green sari being momentarily discarded) and wouldn't they be jealous when they saw Sunil escorting her? All alone with the most eligible bachelor ... imagine that ... it would be all over town. It was all so reckless and wild. It also appealed to her like nothing else did. Today she decided ... today she would throw caution to the winds and revel in it all. Yes ... yes, yes. She was going to do just that.

But ... she frowned again as yet another idea struck her. Wouldn't it be more to her advantage to go the Statesman Club? She could play some tennis and show off her lovely legs. That was the only place she could wear skirts and get away with it. After all she had told her parents several times; you just could not play tennis in a sari or kurta. I was just too silly to contemplate. Of course, she smiled in satisfaction, she knew she had legs that were immensely watchable. They were of the long and silky variety that looked good in skirts and the more miniscule the better. If she hadn't known how good they looked, she probably would not have made such a fuss. Why just last week, Ayush had tried to look up her skirt and when she had reprimanded him hadn't he said "she had legs to die for?"

And later, much later, she just might treat herself to a massage and sauna. For some reason she got tired very easily. Better still, she could get Sunil to drive her to the scenic majesty of the famed Jodhapura mountain range, replete with singing birds and waterfalls and the outing might revive her sagging spirits.

She was lost deep in thought going over and over all her options, there were so many to choose from. The future looked bright and rosy with a sea full of possibilities stretching before her and she felt good. Oh so very very good.

There was a look of expectant excitement on her face and so far gone was she that did not hear Sheila come in. She looked at Mitra deep in thought and said with a tender smile, "dreaming again?"

Mitra jerked back as if she had been hit. "Oh", she said in startled surprise, "my mind must have been elsewhere. I didn't hear you come in."

"Never mind," said Sheila kindly. "You were in your favourite dream world where lesser mortals like me are barred from entry. But come down to reality for a moment please," she said in jest and with a flourish she placed the tray with food and a crystal vase overflowing with bougainvillea from the garden before Mitra. "Well Your Highness, here is your breakfast specially prepared for you by the best possible chef - me!"

By now Mitra was hungry. "What delicious food am I getting today?" she said expectantly. "Croissants, cheese toast or cutlet?"

The smile that was hovering on Mitra's lips was instantly wiped off as she looked at the food set before her. "What is this?" she wailed almost in agony. She picked up the dry bread. "This is as hard as rock," she said in disgust and looks as if it is days old too.

"Look" she said her voice rising, "look it is so hard I cannot even bite it." She sniffed suspiciously at the cheese toast which did not look appetizing in the last. Mitra gave Sheila another glare before picking up the silver pot lying in regal splendour and peered inside surreptitiously – "plain tea" she yelled and looked at Sheila as if betrayed.

"What are you trying to do to me, starve me?" she bellowed in rage. "You should know that I only eat freshly baked croissants or rissoles, squeezed orange juice and brewed coffee. I cannot be expected to eat this kind of rubbish. It is just not possible. Why didn't you ask the other servants?" she went on and with a look of utter disgust she then pushed the tray aside. It fell over he bed and the contents went crashing on to the floor with a deafening sound.

The tea seeped slowly onto the carpet, the cheese toast went flying across the room while the flowers that earlier looked so resplendent now appeared bruised and tried. The vase had of course shattered into a thousand tiny fragments.

Sheila looked at Mitra in exasperation. "Now look what you have gone and done. You are totally impossible. Do you know how hard it is to live with your constant contankerousness, the continual play acting, this reliving of the old days? Pandering to your every whim, every desire and on top of all that not an iota of regard for me, of what I might be feeling and all that I am doing for you. Have you ever thought about that? Have you? Have you?

The words came out in a torrent. They fell over each other in an attempt to get out as quickly as possible. The outburst became hysterical. Years of keeping them in check, of hiding her emotions could no longer be denied. She sobbed it all out.

Mitra just stared at Sheila in bewilderment. Who was this weeping and wailing woman whose hands were flying all over the place and who seemed to be talking total gibberish? It looked … yes it certainly looked like Sheila … but she wasn't sure. Sheila never raised her voice let alone ranted like this, never, absolutely never. And she always smiled … she always, always smiled. No this was not Sheila. This was some horrible stranger. It just had to be.

Mitra's earlier look of defiance and rage was slowly replaced by one of horror and despair. Her face wore a pinched look and she had gone deathly white. Just as suddenly she started to cry, not loudly but soundlessly accompanied by unbearable whimpers that cut straight through the heart.

"I am sorry," Mitra wailed pitifully. "Please forgive me, I did not mean to push the tray away." She looked at Sheila uncomprehendingly. "I forget where we were … I thought … I was … was …" and she added childishly. "I am very very hungry."

For a long moment there was a terrible stillness in the air as Sheila just stood looking at Mitra. Conflicting emotions flickered across her face. Mitra looked so tiny. Such a small figure overwhelmed by the huge four poster bed she sat in. The sheets made from the finest cotton were obviously fraying at the ends and the pillow cases were in no better a shape. She looked at the heavily embroidered Persian carpet now filled with holes she had tried to mend countless times. But it was a losing battle.

She looked at the few pieces of furniture that graced the room. The venetian table lamps replete with angelic cherubs, the pure gold dressing table set, the priceless silver table and chairs studded with precious gems of such impeachable quality that they invariably produced gasps of pure astonishment and envy when seen by others. They were truly antediluvian pieces, each and every one relics of a bygone era. They had been in the family for generations and each had a unique story of its own that only added to its appeal. There is no doubt that they were irreplaceable pieces made by master craftsmen who were no more. One by one they were being sold off at a fraction of their real price to make ends meet.

At other times, Sheila would take the furniture and replace it with questionable pieces from the local bazaar. This was done for Mitra's sake, to keep the house filled while still managing to make some money for them to live on. The house was full of chipped chairs, torn cushions and cracked table lamps.

Sheila once again looked at Mitra's hunched and heaving wiry shoulders. Her graying hair with certain alopecia, the lined and bony hands, the transparent thinness visible beneath the well washed night gown. The face that had once driven men wild and women to unimaginable heights of envy was still beautiful ... but with a beauty that had long since seen its heyday.

She made an indescribably sad picture and it broke Sheila's heart to see her like this. Her grief was unbearable. She felt overwhelmed with guilt. How could she have said all those cruel things? What had got into her? She forgot her angry outburst of a moment ago, her feelings and her anguish no longer seemed to matter. What was important was Mitra and how she was feeling.

She moved towards her and with infinite gentleness took Mitra in her arms. "Its all right my dear, don't cry … please dearest I understand, its all right. I am sorry I said all those nasty things. Please forgive me."

She took Mitra's face in her hands and said, "Look at me. You know how much I love you and always will. You know that don't you?" She said to the still whimpering figure. "You will always be a great lady to me, always. Now please stop crying and try and relax. Here, lie back against the pillows and I will bring you something to eat – I think there is some dry bread left."

# 6

# The Hairdresser

Arti walked into the hotel lobby acknowledging the doorman's over enthusiastic greetings and almost collided with a beautifully coiffeured women. She was in an obvious fluster and was murmuring agitatedly to herself alternately flapping her arms and touching her forehead and her lips and ears in the way Indians do when some sacrilege has been committed. Arti enquired solicitously if there was anything she could do to help.

"What's the matter ... are you all right ...?" were instant reactions.

The woman seemed deeply distressed. She shook her head from side to side murmuring incoherently under her breath ... "I am unclean, I must have a bath straight away. I have been contaminated. Oh God I feel sick. Excuse me, please excuse me" and she literally ran out of the hotel.

For a moment, Arti stared after her and then shrugged her shoulders, the eccentricities of the rich she thought and carried on through the granite filled lobby and up the enormous gold painted staircase. The hotel was one of the most famous in the capital with a wide majestic driveway that ended at an equally imposing entrance. For those who could afford the luxury of five star hotels, this was a favourite. It had the best restaurants, there were six in all, the discotheque was a definite haunt for those who enjoyed dancing and the shops in the arcade were some of the best.

The hotel had an aloofness about it that one could sense the instant you walked through the grand porticos. It was a cultivated trait that the hotel delighted in and never ceased to distress those who were not used to the superficial veneer that was very much a part of the upper strata of Indian life and society.

Naturally a hotel of such distinction also housed a beauty salon that had no rival. The prices were steep but that little fact never got in the way of the client and beautician. This was Arti's first appointment. Her usual hairdresser at another local hotel having gone away on holiday (a definite nuisance) she had decided to venture out instead of making do at home. 'La Beaute', as it was called, came well recommended it. Most of the city's high flying society ladies frequented it. She had booked an appointment earlier in the day using he name of a high powered friend as reference, and had been crisply told by the receptionist that she was extremely lucky, as there had been a cancellation. After giving her name, she was told to arrive on time, at three o'clock on the dot or her appointment would be given to another.

"We are extremely busy as you know and people are coming in all the time. Sofo (the hair stylist she had requested) does not like to be kept waiting" and the phone at the other end went down with a strong click.

Arti smiled to herself as she thought of the conversation. It was already five past and there was sure to be some comments on her tardiness but what the hell … she was the client after all. But she knew that really carried no weight. Hairdressers and beauticians were a most feared and respected breed. They were the ones who made you beautiful and for that magnanimity you were like putty in their hands and you pandered to their whims and not your own despite the fact that you were paying.

As she had feared there was some trouble. Met by glum faces and much unspoken rebuke, she found her appointment had only that very moment been given away to a lady who had been waiting patiently for the past half an hour. Arti tried to keep her patience but she had to have her say. After all it was too, too much.

"You mean to say that I'm just five minutes late and your Sofo or Bofo, whatever you call him could not wait … that's really trying one's patience … I am the client, you have to allow for factors such as traffic, children … some margin. This is beyond anything I have ever heard. It is preposterous."

But Arti knew she was talking to deaf ears, nobody was really listening and their well practiced looks of infinite boredom only incensed her further.

"Well," she said trying to calm down. "If my appointment has already been filled how long will I have to wait or better still was there someone else?"

That provoked some reaction. As she said the words the receptionist looked up, her eyes widening and opened her mouth. For a moment it looked like the words were going to tumble outb ut she seemed to hold them back with superhuman effort and except for a slight shutting and opening of the mouth, not unlike a goldfish, nothing happened.

The next appointment was not cancelled and there were no vacancies at all so it looked highly unlikely that Arti would get her hair done today. She decided being nasty was not going to get her anywhere but arrogance might.

"But I have to get my hair done today, do you understand? I have to get it done today, its very important," she said assertively, images of the party that night floating before her. She knew her hair looked a mess. And with everyone looking their best there was no way she was going without getting it done. "It has to be today. You gave me an appointment and just because I am five minutes late, you have no right to give it away. I want to talk to the management."

"Well ...," said the manageress desperately, wondering at the transformation of the mouse into the lion, "we might have a hairdresser available. I'll just check."

It was a huge parlour, no different from the others dotting the capital, just bigger and snazzier than usual and full to capacity with not a vacant seat in sight. There was a hum of urgency that was palpable. The terrazzo floor was dotted with an abundance of green foliage and flowers such as syringa, oleander, wisteria and the ever popular marigold beckoned invitingly. The parlour fairly crackled with the energy and painstaking devotion that went into making others beautiful.

Arti followed the receptionist to one corner of the parlour. Cut off from the hubbub of the centre it was almost private only it was too much of a cubby hole, more like a nook, to merit such distinction. Having had her hair washed, she flipped desultorily through some magazines and waited patiently for the new hairdresser, Shatru.

What struck Arti right away was how unsure he seemed of himself. Most hairdressers had a certain self-confidence in their ability to make others look well-groomed and this manifest itself in heir walk, their affected talking, their natks and nakharas. So sure of themselves, they felt they owned the place. And in most cases there was a certain truth behind this. For beauty parlours earned and lost their reputations on how good or bad a hairdresser they had.

He seemed ill at ease, almost skittish. His eyes darted all over the place, his hands picked up bottles at random and then put them down just as quickly as he picked them up. It was strange but he appeared almost reluctant to get on with the job. Arti felt bound to ask.

"Are you all right? You look like your mind's elsewhere."

He looked at her directly then. It was patently clear he was making up his mind to say something. He looked around a couple of times to make sure no one was listening and then asked an astonishing question.

"Are you sure you want me to cut your hair?"

Arti stared at him in amazement. What did he meant? At fist Arti answered in the way she was supposed to. She lifted her eyebrows haughtily and said in the superior manner in which inferiors were treated.

"Isn't that what you are supposed to be here for – cutting people's hair?" but then she instantly felt mean seeing him wince slightly.

"Look, is something the matter? I know something is. I mean you are looking distinctly uncomfortable. "Don't you like me?" she said trying to make a joke ... "I don't have any disease you know."

He looked at her directly and said slowly and clearly, "The way people behave you would think I do."

"What? What!" she said disbelievingly.

He moved away from the chair. "I have a disease, a disease you don't really want to know about. And I'm not sure you want me to cut your hair at all."

She swirled around agitatedly pushing off the parlour cloth laid on top of her.

"What do you mean?" she said, her voice rising with the beginnings of hysteria. She put her hands to her face. Hope he doesn't have anything contagious she thought already feeling scratchy.

"Its nothing infectious," he said with a slight grimace as he noted her hands on her face. "Its ... its ..."

"Yes, what ... What?" she almost screamed, her patience tested to the limits.

"Its just that I'm gay and I'm not sure you want me to cut your hair" he said in a straight voice devoid of any emotion. Arti stared at him unable to believe what she had just heard. This couldn't be true. In this day and age? She felt like laughing. The whole thing was ludicrous. And she felt slightly ashamed of her earlier reaction. Finally she found her voice.

"So she said gently, what you are trying to say is you are gay. Right?"

He nodded in affirmation but with a look of apprehension on his face.

She walked over to his side. "So what, just what has that got to do with you cutting my hair?" And then to ease the palpable tension, she said laughingly, "Though you are right about one thing I am definitely not going to catch it, you can be quite sure of that."

Shatru just stared as if mesmerized. He started stuttering. "You ... mean ... you ... don't mind, it ... it doesn't matter to you?" he said incredulously.

"No, it doesn't," said Arti firmly. "I cannot understand why you are making such a big issue about it and why you even bother to tell clients. It's a personal matter and should not be brought into your professional work. What has each got to do with the other anyway?" Without waiting for a reply, she walked back to the chair.

"Now just get on with cutting my hair and don't bother abut what or who you are."

Shatru smiled brightly and Arti was certain he would have liked to have hugged her but refrained from doing so with tremendous self-control. From then onwards everything went smoothly. He treated her like a queen. Nothing, be it the extra magazines or the drink that was not cold enough or the redoing of her hair, nothing was too difficult or too cumbersome for him.

He soon lost the awkwardness that had hung around him like a shroud and became his naturally exuberant and chatty self. He talked non-stop. He was a new recruit and had only been at the parlour for two months having had to move from his previous job because someone had found out he was gay. Once it was out in the open he was shunned, completely. Getting his present job had been a godsend but now it appeared he would not have it for long. Just today a client had found out and had made a real racket.

She was one of their regulars and extremely well known to boot so it looked like he would have to look for another job once again.

I was silent for a moment, thinking how senseless and unjust it was.

"Ever since I started working here she wanted me to do her hair, praising me extravagantly," he said bitterly. She would even wait when he was busy. But once she had found out (during an unguarded moment he had told her he was gay), she had abused him in the presence of everyone so mercilessly and cruelly that he knew he would have to look for another position. As his face suffused with colour, he added," And she had made it sound so dirty, so low down … so abnormal," he said that after the kind of details she had gone into, as if he were a diseased animal, no one in their right mind would accept being touched by him.

"But that is ludicrous," said Arti. "No one has the right to slander you like that. And anyway what has your personal life got to do with anyone? As long as you are good with your work, it should not matter to anyone."

But she knew that was not true. Narrow mindedness was a reflection of a lack of knowledge and there was an abundance of that in the country. She remembered the woman she had seen when entering the hotel. She was well represented in all the major cities. Your typical society matron, plump, in the throes of middle age and well endowed with every possible item of jewellery her ample proportions could support. She was a part of society that made the rules, rules that were inflexible and could not be broken. And they were all the more harsh if one strayed from them. The kind of high society where everyone knew everyone and where anything or anyone out of the norm was a threat and thus dismissed as of no consequence.

Although the change in the climate of the country had brought about a definite openness, the change was too young, too new to have trickled down. Most people were still extremely narrow in their outlook and middle age and money were the worst combination. Clothes designers, artists, musicians, dancers and even hairdressers were looked upon as a different breed. Artistic and arty hence different, wayward, even deviant. But the acceptance was superficial and very limited.

Arti listened to Shatru in silence. Having found a kind and receptive audience, he went on to tell her of all the offences he and his kind were made to suffer. The viciousness that was rife in a society where tolerance was not viewed favourably. That anything which differed too radically from the mainstream was to be treated with mistrust and prejudice. For by being different it could never be accepted, could never be right. Because it touched some nerve centers that said that what was the norm was safe and what was different was deviant. And there could never be any compromise on that.

"People say I am dirty and will not allow me to touch them. Do I look dirty to you, do I?" he said in a shrill indignation. "Just because I am different. People treat me like a criminal. They laugh behind my back, mimic me continuously and treat me with revulsion. It is just not fair but worse it is not right."

Despite Shatru's non-stop talking and avid gesticulating, Arti's hair looked superb once he had finished. It fell in all the right places and the rinse he had suggested suited her. She was genuinely pleased at what she saw. She congratulated him openly in front of the other staff and clients, knowing he needed the reassurance. She tipped him as lavishly as was possible without getting too sentimental. "I'll be back, wait and see. I'll be back."

Arti arrived at the parlour the following week without an appointment but secure in the knowledge that Shatru would not turn her away. Her request for him brought many blank looks and much whispering. When she confronted the manageress and demanded to know what had happened, she was not at all surprised to hear that he was no longer with the parlour.

She was incredibly saddened to hear of his dismissal. Nevertheless, she was disgusted with their attitude. Nobody seemed to know where he had gone and neither were they keen to discuss the matter. He was just a fag who didn't really matter. His obvious talent was of no consequence in the face of his crime. He was gay. And that was simply that.

# 7

## The Butler

Ajay was determined to be rich and his determination soon paid off. As soon as he made his first crore from a scrap deal, graduating from 'kabadhiwallah' to 'scrap businessman', he and his wife moved into one of the most expensive houses in the capital. It was built by the finest architects and an interior designer of worldwide repute was called in. The house had everything that was expensive. Beautiful Italian marble, venetian chandeliers and an all wooden staircase imported piece by piece from an impoverished Duke's house in the English countryside. But that was not all. There was a magnificent four poster bed that belonged at one time to an infamous gangster and added a sense of black history which the owner delighted in. The carpets strewn all over the house were indeed quite priceless, selected from different corners of the world – Ancient Iran, India and China. Each woven flower petal, village scene or a face had a story to tell to the discerning. The furniture was for the most part antique pieces as was much of the art. There was no doubt that the house was magnificent and both husband and wife enjoyed the experience of living amidst such beauty without really understanding the value except in purely monetary terms.

They acquired a chief from one of the swanky five star hotels who succumbed with the help of an enormous bribe;

a car of his own! They added a vast retinue of servants, all the necessary appendages that signified they had arrived. They then went further and hired a butler, Madhav, an anachronism in this day and age but a throwback to the Raj, and in today's world another example of how the rich lived, a testament to their whim and the power of money.

Having created the right kind of ambience with the necessary props, they went about climbing the social ladder in an attempt to meet other moneyed people. Towards this goal, dinner parties were hosted thrice a week to meet the 'right' kind of people. But somehow these parties were never very successful. Perhaps it was due to the kind of people they were themselves. They were never really comfortable with those they had invited. Invariably feeling inferior on every score and never managing to quite enter the conversations that ringed with grown associations and shared references.

After spending a lot of money and getting nowhere, Ajay realised something was drastically wrong. He was still not invited to the most exclusive parties, the so-called crème de la crème affairs, nor did he attract the kind of business he was seeking despite his thriving companies. In fact, if anything, he was beginning to feel used. These people all seemed to come to his parties more for Madhav's sake, to drink his fancy wines and eat his fine food and sometimes 'just for the sake of it' but never really to meet the hosts.

"What is wrong with my parties?" Ajay asked the butler, Madhav who had in the course of the past few months become something of a confidant. From the very start the two had hit it off. But it was a strange union. To look at, Madhav, was not unlike a Greek God. He was tall and slim, muscular in all the right places and incredibly handsome. He had a high forehead, patrician nose and a jaw that was strong and sexy especially as it had a deep cleft. But it was his eyes that held your attention. They were on the smaller side, dark green with long eyelashes. And they seemed to look directly into your soul. Nobody quite knew where he came from. But there were rumours to the effect that he was the black sheep of a particularly royal family, hence the style, the suave manners and general air of breeding and of course the fact that he seemed to know everybody. He was strong of character and always managed to get his own way. Some said he was a quiet strategist who saw each situation as it should be much before it had actually taken place and then worked towards the goal. There was no doubt he was highly intelligent. With a combination like that, he was simply irresistible. Women of course could not get enough of him!

Ajay, on the other hand, was short, pot-bellied and uninteresting to look at. But for some unfathomable reasons these two shared a tremendous rapport. It was very unlike a master-servant relationship. But then nobody could imagine treating Madhav with anything but equal respect. Somehow he commanded it.

In this master-servant combine, however, it would appear that Madhav was more in command while Ajay was the subservient of the two. But more than that, what was really unusual was how very physical the relationship was. The two men were always touching each other; whether it was slapping one another on the back, holding hands or just hugging each other for no accountable reason. To all it appeared far too friendly and intimate. It was a strange relationship but neither seemed to care.

Thus, when Ajay asked Madhav what was wrong with his parties he knew he would get an honest answer and certainly, Madhav did not mince his words.

"The problem likes with Mrs. Kapur."

Ajay stared at him thunderstruck. Whatever else he expected it was certainly not this.

"Why ... why, what do you mean ... what is wrong with her?"

He was blunt and to the point. "She has no class, no looks, no style in fact nothing. Your wife should be an asset to you but instead she is detracting from all you are doing."

Ajay was upset. 'This time he's gone too far,' he thought to himself. But he began to watch his wife carefully. That very night they had another party. She was wearing a shimmering French chiffon sari that had just arrived from London and for which he had paid a bomb. Her blouse had puffed sleeves with little bows at the end. Her shoes were bright red "to match the red specks in her sari."

She was wearing a multi-coloured bow in her hair and had bedecked herself with an enormous amount of jewellery everywhere. There was not a portion of her skin that was not covered and she looked like a Christmas tree. He privately thought she looked good but he also noticed none of the other ladies were wearing anything as shiny or as bright. Their attire consisted of sober prints and bright borders. Kanjeevarams, Pathanis, Tangails – these seemed to be the appropriate choice. Perhaps Madhav had been right.

The jewellery that he had recently presented her with now looked a trifle over done. The enormous jharao piece hanging from her beck and ears seemed to stand out too much. He craned his neck and stared at the other ladies in the room. Pearls and diamonds were the order of the day. Of course, there were some women wearing jharao jewellery, but they somehow seemed appropriate. Mrs. Kapur began to look increasingly like a stuffed parantha filled to capacity and oozing from all sides.

He gulped his drink down all the while to be agreeing with what the tiresome Mr. Singh said (he was after all the largest manufacturer of air conditioners in the country). He knew the rules of the game well by now and would agree with anything he said.

Over the next couple of weeks, Ajay watched his wife like a hawk. At first he couldn't make up his mind (not being sophisticated himself) but eventually he decided that Madhav was right. He had to be.

Mrs. Kapur had no inkling of the conversation that had transpired between the two nor was she aware of her husband's thoughts.

Subtly he began to change her image. When she liked a piece of jewellery that was actually horrendous, he would somehow steer her away from it by buying her two pieces instead of one. Her clothes were no longer loud but tasteful and elegant. He engaged teachers in etiquette, general knowledge and social skills and put her through rigorous training. Madhav, of course, involved and consulted in everything.

And slowly she changed. But in the process she changed so much that she no longer found him compatible. Everything he did was wrong. The way he matched his clothes; the colours were too loud and the type of clothes he wore were too flashy. The way he spoke with an affected accent, the way he ate his food and talked while it was still in his mouth. His habit of always discussing money was "common". All this began to grate on her nerves. "We are just not compatible" became a refrain he heard constantly. The tables were truly turned.

But the strange fact was that Ajay did not seem to mind in the least. Their marriage was falling apart, the distance between them was growing, but he remained exactly the way he was - loud and flashy. Madhav remained his inscrutable self, no one really ever knew what he was thinking. But his friendship with Ajay continued to be as strong as ever.

Suddenly a bombshell occurred. Mrs. Kapur and

Madhav left town together. The while city rocked with the shocking news that they had eloped together. And she had asked for a divorce. But somehow no one was surprised. Despite his enormous wealth, Ajay was no match for the butler who all the women secretly fantasized about and all the men secretly envied. "She actually ran away with the butler of all people. But he was handsome!" "What a tart. I always suspected her. There was something not quite right about her, well when compared to Ajay anyone is better and he was quite a man!" The menfolk were less disparaging. "The lucky devil," "I wonder if they took all those jewels with them," and so forth.

The butler and the lady were top party conversation for quite a while before things started to quieten down. Just as the city was beginning to return to normal came another bomb shell. The butler had returned and was back at the house. Alone.

Alone? Where was the lady of the house, what had he done to her? Maybe he had used all her money and dumped her, maybe he had run off with all the money. Perhaps she had thrown him out ... well, no ... no that was not possible! Some said he had tired of her ... after all, despite her recent transformation she was too gauche for his sophisticated ways. He needed someone with more refinement. Some even said that she had dumped him. She had outgrown him and moved on to better and higher things. Well, what did it matter, the main thing was he was back.

All at once Ajay's empty house was packed with visitors and once again there were parties till early dawn, with expensive wine and delicious food. Everything went back to the way it had been before. But there was one major difference. While Ajay and his wife had presided at previous parties, now it was Ajay and Madhav who lorded it over and as a couple hand in hand, very much together in the grand scheme of things!

# 8

# Man about the House

Tara was happy and it showed min many different ways, in the involuntary smile that lit up her face periodically in the numerous out-of-key tunes she hummed softly to herself, in the little dance steps she could not resist and in her hands as they deftly and with practiced ease busied themselves with the cooking. The kitchen was her sanctuary and in its environs she found an enveloping peace. It was warm and welcoming and pleasing to the eye, with its rust coloured mosaic tiles, vegetable patterned wall paper and plants perched atop cupboards and hanging from the ceiling. There was an old fireplace besides which were two well worn cushioned chairs in a cheery chintz print, a vivid rug with an Aztec motif and many dried flower decorations. The kitchen had a farm house feeling that relaxed those who entered its portals.

Jars of all kinds of condiments, jams and spices were neatly laid in ros and the fridge was always well stocked with grapes, melons or the fruit of the season. Here Tara could immerse herself in the preparation of a favourite dish; dwelling on each ingredient, feeling their magic with her hands, inhaling the aroma and closing her eyes in ecstasy as if their very aroma reached some part of her soul. And they had to be fresh. Anything less would not do. Thus the packaged variety was never seen in her kitchen. Checking and rechecking each item and then losing herself so completely in her most treasured hobby that cooking invariably took longer than it ought to. But it was always worth the wait. The dishes that were presented ultimately were both a work of art to behold and the taste was indescribably delicious – a connoisseur's delight.

In the kitchen, Tara cut herself off from the rest of the world, any problems or worries sorted themselves out as her hands worked magically and her thoughts moved on to other realms. Not that she was a day dreamer but just that she liked to do her thinking in an atmosphere that was of her own choosing. Tara somehow did not belong to this world. She lived elsewhere, in her mind, in a place of her own choosing, only venturing now and then because she had to.

Tara was a little woman, no moe than four feet and ten inches, and a real beauty. A small retrousse nose, perfectly arched eyebrows that owed nothing to artifice below which were eyes; the colour of the sea. At times blue and green, at times brown but always wide and luminous, innocent and childlike. A wide forehead and well defined lips completed the picture. But apart from being such a refined beauty, Tara was a lovely person, a trifle shy, but affectionate and full of warmth for everyone. This was apparent in the joy others took from seeing her and invariably some friend or the other dropped in to have a chat. Perhaps it was her small frame, her defenceless look, her innocence, or then again may be it was all three. But whatever it was, she inspired deep protective instincts from those who loved her.

Today she had decided to cook fesanjun, a winter Iranian dish she had learned from a close Persian friend when her husband had been posted in the country. It was a very special dish, for it brought back several happy memories of their stay there, that were startingly vivid ... like the warmth of shared meals, of dropping in accidentally and still being welcomed. Memories of winter nights and warm fires, and exchanged confidences. The smell of the barbecue and much laughter. A cherished time, yes a very special time.

Tara had become something of an expert at this dish, having mastered it authentically and in the process it had become a popular meal with the family. First she grated the onions, tears rushing to her eyes as the acidity from the onion juice stung and Nayantara, hr daughter entering the kitchen at just that moment, rusher to her side in concern.

"Why didn't you call me to grate the onion, look at your eyes, mama, you just sit down and relax, you shouldn't be doing this, please listen to me. Sit down, sit down and let me do it quickly."

Nayantara was as ugly as her mother was beautiful. A broad flat nose dominated her other features which were so unremarkable that the only thing people noticed was the nose. All her life she had lived with this handicap, more pronounced when people stared disbelievingly at he mother. It had, however, produced no grudge or resentment in Nayantara. On the contrary, she idolized her mother.

Her mother's beauty and delicate mien had developed feelings of protection in the child. As far as she could remember, she had always wanted to look after her mother. It had a lot to do with the early morning and late right rituals of bedtime stories and being told you were loved. It was demonstrated in affectionate cuddles and much hugging and kissing. And Nayantara blossomed under such love. And though the bedtime stories had changed to shared confidences, the tucking in still remained and the kissing still continued with Nayantara more of the protector and her mother the recipient.

As Nayantara tried to take the grater from her mother's hands, she protested gently. "No you listen silly," she laughed lovingly, do not fuss so. I am making fesanjun, you know your father's favourite dish, and I want to make it all myself."

Then scooping the grated onion into the deep pan, she failed to see the look of concern and odd side glance her daughter gave her.

"Oh?" was all Nayantara could say in a seemingly nonchalant manner.

"Now let me cook," her mother said looking at her affectionately, "it is getting late and your father will be here soon."

Tara seemed to forget about hr as she immersed herself in the cooking. Nayantara stood looking at her mother. She had lost a lot of weight, she noted, she had dark circles under her eyes which she had made an attempt to hide with a foundation cream that stood out a mile and her collarbones protruded through hr blouse. She made an incoherent sound and bit her lips. She stood at the entrance of the kitchen for a long while with a strange look on her face and then rushed out abruptly but Tara, sublimely unaware of anything except the food preparation in front of her failed to notice her daughter's tense departure.

Soon the chicken was frying on low heat while Tara got the sauce ready. It was a sweetish mixture of pomegranate concentrate and walnuts. In no time, the ingredients were all heaped together and the sauce was bubbling gentley. She then put the soaked rice on a slow fire and left to have a shower.

An hour later, looking incredibly pretty in a peach cotton sari with a purple border and patterned blouse, she set the table and called out that dinner was ready and they would be eating soon. On hearing hr mother's dulcet voice, Nayantara entered the room with a look of apprehension. The dining table was transformed from its usually everyday look to one of festive elegance. She saw that the special damask tablecloth had been used and the venetian crockery was laid out which was something very rare. It was only used on special occasions when they had something to celebrate. The table was dominated by a vase of spectacular irises, the profusion and abundance of the yellow and purple colour adding a vividness to the setting. Seeing her mother's smiling face, she pulled herself together and sat down ready to eat.

"Okay mother, I am ready for the great dish," she said.

"But," Tara protested, "we must wait. We can't eat now, your father is not here yet."

Nayantara stared at her mother in total amazement. "Why did you call me then? You just said dinner was ready." Her mouth stayed open and she wanted to say more but no words came out. With a slight shake of her head, she changed her mind and said instead, her tone terse: "Papa is always late on Tuesdays, you know that, he wouldn't want us to wait for him."

"I know, I know," said her mother. "But let us wait just a bit, you know how your Papa likes eating with us. And you'll also be able to talk to him. That would make him very happy," she said pleadingly.

Then catching sight of her daughter's strained face, she quickly added, "but if you are very hungry maybe we should start." Nayantara seized her chance and agreed at once, "Yes let us."

Still, her mother hesitated and much to her chagrin asked her to be patient and wait just a while longer. Nayantara grimaced in response but decided to humour her mother. They waited for over an hour. Tara sat calmly and happily humming to herself. Nayantara tried to kill time by flipping through a magazine but she put it down after a few minutes without reading a word. Then she looked through hr CD collection to put on some music but out of the hundreds of CDs she could find nothing for the moment. She switched on the television but each programme seemed more inane than the other. She was becoming increasingly tense and agitated and finally no longer able to contain herself, she shouted in frustration.

"How can you sit there waiting for someone who is not going to come? You know Papa died a year ago, he's dead, he's dead, don't you understand? He's dead, so stop kidding yourself. It is time you faced reality, so lets just get on and eat," she sobbed tearfully.

Tara was aghast. She stood up drawing herself to her full height and shouted back, "Have you gone mad, have you lost leave of your senses? What ever is the matter with you, how can you bring yourself to tell such pernicious untruths, such blasphemy, such horrible lies?"

She shook her with all her strength. "I could slap you for saying such a vile thing about your father." Then seeing Nayantara's tearful face, she took her gently in her arms and questioned hr sadly, "my darling what has upset you and made you say such vile things? It is so unlike you. How can you say such a grotesque thing like this? And what is more about your own father. I just cannot believe it. This is too much, just too much."

It was Nayantara's turn to stare at her mother in disbelief. She couldn't believe what she was hearing but decided to hold her tongue and refused to say anything further, but just wept miserably into her handkerchief.

Tara looked at her daughter helplessly. "Sometimes I just don't understand you," she said in exasperation, "but you are right it is late ..." she hesitated for a few moments, "... we won't wait any longer, we'll leave the food for your father in the kitchen, he can heat it when he comes home later."

They ate in silence broken only by the occasional sounds of laughter from outside. The fesanjun looked extremely appetizing, lightly brown with the pomegranate seeds shining through and the walnuts adding to the crunchy texture. It was delicious but both their appetites had waned. The exchange earlier had left them dispirited with the result that they both toyed with their food, not eating much.

Nayantara was tired and upset. Her mind was whirling with a multitude of thoughts rushing at her from all sides, pricking her mind like thousands of little needles. She felt confused and uncertain. When would her mother face the truth? And she wondered for how long she could keep up with this, this act of deception. She was not sure how long she could keep up a brave face.

Her mother lost in her own thoughts said very little. The meal was over soon and they cleared the table together each in their own separate world. By some unspoken mutual consent they decided to retire early.

Nayantara found it difficult to sleep. The electricity had gone off and she could feel the sweat trickling down her back and her knee joints. She tossed from side to side wondering how long the power cut would last. "It could last the whole night," she said out loud. And it probably would, she thought in anger. Didn't it go every night? She hadn't had a decent night's sleep for the past week and she felt miserable and irritated. Though she should be used to it by now. Having tossed about for another hour she decided to have a glass of cold milk.

On entering the kitchen, the first thing she saw was a plate set on the sideboard, filled with rice and fesanjun waiting to be heated for her father. She couldn't believe it, it was like some horrible nightmare. Oh dear God. When was all this going to end? When would the denouement take place? What was wrong with her mother, her dearest most precious, beautiful and gentle mother?

In pure frustration, she found herself sobbing gently, half laughing at the absurdity of the situation, half in pain and despair. How was she ever going to convince her mother that her father was dead? For how long could she exist in a world where he was always on business, hence the reason why he was never at home? The third Tuesday of every month always brought this emotional upset. It was, in fact, the day he had died in the car accident. But that fatal day seemed to be erased from her mother's mind. Instead, he was not seen by others but existed only in the world of her mother's making. Knowing no one was going to eat fesanjun, Nayantara opened the fridge and put both the rice and the fesanjun back in their respective dishes and washed the plate.

Next morning, she awoke to the fan whirring above her. She couldn't remember when she had fallen asleep but it had been after hours of deep thinking and staring at the ceiling above. Thank God, she thought as she heaved herself out of bed. Her mother's louder than usual humming, struck her as unusual; it was not the soft under the breath humming she was used to hearing. It had a lilt of happiness that was unexpected after yesterday's events and that was most unlike her mother.

"Did you see your father?" Tara asked her daughter as she entered the room. Nayantara shook her head wearily, oh no, she thought, not again. It only happens on Tuesdays, why had she lapsed so soon.

Her mother took no notice of her silence. "Your father arrived late last night, he slept in the spare bedroom so as not to disturb me. He ate all his fesanjun and even washed the dishes she chirped happily. "I think he went out for a walk but he should be back in time for breakfast. I miss him so much," she broke for a moment, tears smarting her eyes and her voice wobbled dangerously, "I wish he could stay home all the time." Then she brightened up, "but he's here now and I had better go and get breakfast ready."

Nayantara looked at her mother. Here was a different person from the one she had left the night before. Before her stood a woman who was positively glowing. For her, everything was in its place as it should be and as far as as she was concerned her husband was alive and well. She seemed convinced of that fact. It was all too much … it was just too unbelievable. Nayantara opened her mouth to speak and then shut it again. What could say? Was there any point in saying anything? That she had put the food away last night and washed the dish. No, her mother would not believe her, worse it would upset her again and Nayantara could not bear that. She would just have to keep quiet about the dishes. She turned away in utter despair. What should she do? In frustration, she put her knuckles in her mouth and chewed on them. Would she believe her or even listen to her if she told her mother?

But it was wrong ... it was wrong to let her mother live like this, in total ignorance of reality and really, anyway, for how long would it last? How long before she came to her senses and realized what the truth was? By then maybe the reality would be too much for her to endure. What if ... what if the shock of it all became too much for her. What would happen then? Yes, she realized she had to make her mother understand now. Right now. In fact, it was imperative she do so before something terrible happened that was irreversible.

She turned back towards her mother dreading what she had to say but knowing she had to tackle the problem head one. Her voice was flat and intensely compulsive.

"Ma, listen to me, and listen to me clearly. Please try and be brave and try and understand, truly understand what I am about to say. Papa is dead. He died last year in a car accident. Don't you remember, you were with him ... we both were ... "look, look at your hand" and she pulled her mothr's arm forward, "look, look at the mark you got in the accident," pointing to the ugly gash that would always remain. "Do you remember now, do you?"

Her mother moaned. But remained silent and just looked at her daughter with sad eyes overflowing with tears. Nayantara could not bear the agonized look that had replaced the smile on her mother's face. She felt her heart twist inside itself and rushed to put her arms around her and hugged her hard.

Determined to do what was right, she took her mother's trembling hands in her own and holding on to them tightly said, "You must face the truth. There are only both of us left now but don't worry. I'll always be here to look after you. Always." Her voice faltered for a few seconds but then took on a conviction that came through in the confident manner in which she said "always".

It was her mother's turn to take her in her arms and rock her gently. "Oh, my love, my child, my dearest child," she said painfully, "when will you understand, when will you understand?"

A few minutes passed by with mother and daughter wrapped in each other's arms. The silence was broken by a slamming door and then a familiar manly voice from upstairs floated down … where are my slippers … ? Tara … did I leave them downstairs again?

# 9

# Death

Jayanti bai walked home quickly, her anklets tinkling, bangles clinking and the multi-coloured glass encrusted ghagra swaying from side to side as it tried to keep pace with her frenetic stride. It was past midnight and the roads were deserted except for the lone dog, hungry and still scavenging from the numerous rubbish heaps that kept appearing all over the city unchecked, spreading their vast testacles and gradually establishing a monopoly. The street lights were so dim they were of virtually no help. Most were in their twilight years, rusty and of ancient technology, testament of another era that badly needed to haul itself into the 21st century. They existed because they were there and no one had bothered to replace them, or if someone had the middle man had already taken his share and an obsolete design was replaced with another equally ancient apparatus. Thus their insufficient rays shone down on the dark roads with indifference.

Jayanti bai was exhausted. She has always tired by the end of the day. There was nothing unusual in that, but recently, especially in the last few weeks, she was beginning to tire more easily. Not did she feel well. She was always lethargic, did not enjoy talking to others, in fact seemed to shun their company. She intuitively knew there was something wrong with her ... something drastically wrong

… it was almost as if her life was slowly being sucked away … one horrifying disease had come to mind … those who had seen it before said she had the symptoms … but she had neither the time nor the money to find out. In truth she was too scared to face what she already knew in her heart.

It had been a particularly hard day. She worked as an assistant to the cook and was cleaner-cum-washer-woman-cum-maid, in the house of an affluent businessman earning Rs. 650 per month. Meals were included in her salary but seemed that the wealthier the household the more miserly the rations. Food was never exciting and she had to make do with stale food and left overs that were inadequate. There had been a big party that very night which meant more work and not a whisper about overtime pay.

Mrs. Khanna, hr employ was a mean woman, who cared nothing for her servants but only that the household chores should be done. The food for the party had been exquisite, for the cook was something of a connoisseur but unfortunately Jayanti bai had not tasted a morsel of it. After catering to a guest list of thirty, she had to be content with yesterday's leftovers.

As she felt the faint rumbling in her stomach she sighed deeply and rubbed her hand over the protesting area. She knew she was being short changed. But what was she to do? She had to make ends meet. Domestic jobs were not all that easy to come by and at least the memsahib did not ill treat her. She had complained to her earlier in the day, thinking back to their conversation.

It could not go on like this for much longer, the long hours, inadequate pay and insufficient food. Her face was darker now with remembered resentment. It was only misplaced loyalty and gratitude that kept her from leaving. But that did not mean that Mrs. Khanna take advantage of her. Mrs. Khanna had seemed nervous at that moment and tried to pacify her but just then Mr. Khanna had emerged from his study, roaring in anger.

"Couldn't a man ever had a little peace? He had heard enough of her sob story, her bak-bak?" And he had gone back to the study with a scowl on his face.

But she would not give up. She certainly did not need to work so late in the night of the kind of pay they gave her. She would try again tomorrow. She sighed deeply. But now she was willing to take whatever was available. Survival did not leave that many options open.

She always made it a point to complete her work as quickly as possible in the evenings for she knew the dangers of walking home in the dark. But today that plan had not worked out as expected. Just as she had finished the last of the dishes a whole group of the memsahib's fancy guests arrived which meant more work. Re-heating the food, waiting for them to finish eating and washing the dishes all over again. And so here she was trudging back at almost one o'clock in the morning.

Home was a small decrepit shanty hut, if it could be called that. It was constantly being torn down, which was very easy to do because it was made of cardboard, some bricks, polythene and woven bamboo-like grass. Construction workers and people who represented all kinds of big interests took advantage of these makeshift properties. Electricity was provided by the local 'dada' who squeezed an exorbitant fee from them. He meanwhile stole the electricity by attaching an illegal wire to an existing official one. Here water was scarce and there were no toilets. Thus the area had a constant smell of cow dung and human faeces hanging over it.

The houses were no different from the millions of other dilapidated cardboard homes on the roadside that were virtually indistinguishable from the others. And of no consequence to those whose world was far removed from it. To them it represented dirt, filth, the seedy and polluted face of the country but for Jayanti bai and her family it was home.

The darkness of the night and dead silence that hung in the air was scaring and the shadows seemed particularly menacing. In a hurry to get home, Jayantib ai had taken a short cut, something she would never normally do. It was a narrow little lane, that stank of urine and rubbish. During the day it bustled with life but lost its vivacity as the light faded. It was now alive with rats scuttling across from every corner. And so deep in thought was she that it was quite some time before she realized she was being followed. She started sweating, her heart pounding loudly and she felt apeculiar weakness in her bones.

"Who's there?" she yelled out in fright.

The fright was always prevalent. It came before actual realization dawned. To be frightened, to feel your hands become cold and clammy, to feel the acceleration of your heartbeat like a train whistling without breaks. To feel your body go hot and cold, icy cold – all because you are frightened. This feeling becomes part of you, an invisible cloak hanging around you – always ready to engulf you in its folds. This feeling dogged all those who had no recourse to justice. A result of living and facing the harsh facts of life the poor were always burdened with. Numerous incidents were submerged, with no promise of ever seeing the light of the day.

Jayanti bai stopped in her tracks and turned round to stare into the eyes of a policeman. The apparent fright with which she looked at him did not however diminish on seeing a custodian of the law standing opposite her. She thought he looked respectable enough but you never could tell. And that was the problem. You tended to trust them and were always let down. Numerous ugly incidents flashed through her mind. Last year Shakti behan had been brutally assaulted, and then there was Naina ji who had killed herself because of the shame. And ... and ... the incident of Shanti bai came to mind. Just a few days ago she had been raped by some local businessman and the matter had been hushed up because he had greased some palms. But what about all the women who had to live with the stigma for the rest of their lives? What about them? They were abused and then cast aside and would face countless such hardships before life closed upon them.

Jayanti bai knowing the futility of running decided to confront the man pursuing her.

"Why are you following me?" she said.

She was dismayed to notice how squeaky and unsure her voice sounded, unlike its usual strident sound that was strong and confident, as she was wont to portray.

The policeman said nothing. He calmly lit his bidi, inhaled and grinned, his paan-stained teeth displayed prominently. He slowly and with precise movements started hitting his lathi against the palms of his hands in a most menacing manner.

Jayanti bai, despite her fright tried to keep her wits about her. She looked around wildly hoping to see someone, anyone, she could call to come to her aid. But there was not a soul on the streets. She thought of shouting loudly but the moment the thought came to her, she recognized its futility. The policeman would not stand by idly and even if she did manage a few yells there was no one to heed her cries for help.

She instinctively knew what he wanted. He didn't need to spell it out. By now he was looking her over suggestively and scratched his groin in an obscene manner. She saw it in the quick glance he gave as he looked around him to make sure all was safe.

As he moved forward she said threateningly: "Don't you dare lay a finger on me, do you understand? You will regret it."

But he brushed aside her threats and laughed loudly.

What did any man want she thought to her bitterly? A little bit on the side for the sake of variety. A little something to keep him going. The sad fact was that in such cases it usually did not m atter who the victim was. For those imprecise moments the victim, any victim was perfect. After they had done the dirty deed the victim became nothing but rubbish. Animals she thought to herself. They were all animals willing to devour anyone that came along.

He did not see her as she was; the lines on her face and the well past middle age spread, all he saw was woman. Nor did he see the intelligence in the face, the strong jaw, the liquid eyes that were large and enquiring. He saw past the fact that she was so obviously twice his age. In fact old enough to be his mother. He saw none of these things. She was just a piece of flesh that was available and he was more than ready."

"Let us go," he said roughly and before she knew it he had taken her arm and was pulling her to a shaded area near by.

"You must listen to me," Jayanti bai cried out in desperation. "I am not well, I am a very sick woman."

The policeman acted as if he had not heard and she screamed frantically: "What is wrong with you, you filthy animal? I am telling you for your own good. What do you want with a diseased body like mine?"

For just a moment the officer seemed to falter. He then dragged her under the one solitary light in the lane and looked at her face. "Be careful," he cautioned himself. "I don't want to be stuck with some dirty disease. Who knows where these women have been and what infections they have picked up?"

"What is wrong with you?" he asked Jayanti bai shaking her roughly. All a weeping Jayanti bai in her hysterical state could reply was, "don't touch me. I am very ill, I am very ill. Don't touch me. You will regret it." She kept repeating this incoherently. But the policeman having had a good look at her had reassured himself that there was nothing wrong with her. She seemed fine. There was enough meat on her bones in which to bury himself nicely. And hadn't he heard these refrains couched in different terms from countless women before? He had to admit this one was more ingenious but ... why was he wasting his time ... who cared anyway ... here he was, still going strong.

As Jayanti bai struggled with him her breasts came in contact with his hands and he felt a strong sense of arousal. Her breasts were unexpectedly large and thrust out against his chest. The waft of womanly smell that emanated from her body was more than he could bear. He peered at her closely and decided she was lying. She looked so good and the struggle was all the more inviting. And he began tearing her clothes like a mad man as his desired surged within him.

Jayanti bai continued to fight him off, shouting and abusing him all the while. But it only seemed to excite him further. He pushed Jayanti bai against the ground and slapped her twice telling her to keep her mouth shut. He extricated her breasts from her blouse, pinching and squeezing them with delight. He then grabbed both her hands almost crushing them with his strength and pushed them above her head. She was terrified by now, her face deathly pale and she tried to pull away from him as he moved closer and closer. Laughing evilly at her evident reluctance, he pushed her ghagra up to her waist. Fully exposed she closed her eyes in shame while his hands went all over her body, his mough touching her face and emitting alcohol fumes that threatened to suffocate her. He viciously thrust himself in her. The act itself was no big deal. After a few cruel shoves he could contain himself no longer and in his intense excitement he bit deeply into her shoulder drawing blood. His movements became more urgent and in seconds with a shuddering sigh ejaculated inside her. It was over very quickly.

She looked at the blood around his mouth, obviously from the bite on her shoulder and knew he was doomed. She was shaking all over, she could not get hr teeth to stop chattering, her mouth was dry and her body ached. She felt completely violated; dirty and abused. She was exhausted and wished she could crawl somewhere and hide. She wanted to yell out, to hit the man ... to do something ... to tell him the truth ... but she hadn't the energy and she lay lifeless and broken.

Once finished he could not wait to get away from the scene. He looked around him wildly to make sure there were no witnesses. Having simply thrust her away from him, he zipped himself and was about to hurry on his way without even a second glance. But something about her silence made him turn back. There was something ... he could not put his finger on it ... could not quite put a name to it ... it was almost as if she knew some secret. Now that the deed was done, she seemed almost, almost pleased. He shook his head in disbelief. But no, that could not be. It was impossible. Looking at her he felt himself shiver slightly. She did not appeared cowed or broken. Instead her expression suggested immense satisfaction. Maybe, he thought, she was one of 'those' women who actually enjoyed the struggle and forced intercourse with strangers. But then he dismissed the idea immediately. No, somehow she didn't appear the type. Her struggle and reluctance had been genuine.

He turned around and slowly walked back towards her still lying body. Yes he hadn't been mistaken. There was a strange knowing look in her eyes and a half smile on her lips. What the hell was she smiling about? A feeling of disquiet came over him.

"What are you smiling about?" he yelled savagely. "Are you mad or what?"

There was no response and in fact her smile became broader. Taken aback the policeman wondered if in fact she was mad. But she certainly did not look it. She had about her the knowledge of some secret he didn't and he felt at a distinct disadvantage. The earlier satisfaction as washed away in the sea of apprehension.

Jayanti bai refused to say anything and just continued to smile. With a strong sense of misgiving, he stumbled away.

A few years later there was a short note in the newspape that a well known and respected policeman called Kumar had died. Nothing specific was mentioned and till recently the cause of his death is not known. Enquiries by friends and relatives similarly struck a dead end. And for a while, he became a hot subject for gossip and speculation among fellow officers. And as is always the case other interesting incidents that made for better gossip took precedence and soon Kumar's name was no longer mentioned.

But someone in the know might have noticed that about the same time another death occurred and put two and two together. It was that of Jayanti bai, a poor maid who drifted from job to job with no fixed locale. Her death unlike Kumar's however hit the headlines. It was part of a report by the World Health Organisation. The report said AIDS was fast spreading among woman and that by the turn of the century out of nearly sixteen million infected women, four million would have died. You see, Jayanti bai had died of AIDS.

# 10

# The Party

All his life Sardar Amarinder Singh had been browbeaten by his wife Surinder. He was not a particularly weak man nor did he suffer from a nervous disposisiton, rather his wife to whom he was quite devoted was to put it in simple words a nag. And she was not your average run-of-the-mill nag, nor was she a volatile nag who once having nagged would seek retribution. Rather she was the dawn-to-dust nag, who whined the whole day and night and in doing so wore down her adversary.

Her husband was the perfect recipient of such nagging and the years of constantly being told to do this or that had left their mark. He had an air of suffering about him, a weariness of the brow that was instantly discernible and at once understood upon meeting his wife.

Too much nagging and he was apt to go into such a state that his hands would start trembling and his speech would become disjointed. "Your at it again," he would say. But that was in extreme cases. Most of the time it was not overtly obvious but nevertheless it was there and a constant reminder to Amarinder Singh of his own inadequacies against his wife.

And thre was no doubt about it, it was getting worse. More than a few minutes of being nagged at and the trembling would start. Some days were worse than others because Surinder would harp on one subject for the whole day and if she had not got a satisfactory result then it would run into the next day, and the next, sometimes running into days.

Over the years, Amarinder had begun to believe that Surinder actually enjoyed the nagging and derived immense satisfaction from the fact the 'it' got to him. He could see it in the silly way she twittered and when her hands went flapping all over. And when she went 'my' in that mocking voice, he knew she had scored a real victory. This was her way of getting at him. He never knew why or what he had done to make her act the way she did. Mind you he had no concrete evidence that she enjoyed seeing him become a nervous wreck, it was just a feeling that had built up over the years.

He never voiced his feelings. To do so would be an acknowledgement of his weakness, a sure sign that this wife had got to him. He could never let her know that. During the days of their courtship she had never manifested any such tendencies and during the early years of their marriage, when he was young and strong, he had even told her to shut up a number of times but he had to admit those were few and far between and she had over the years, gradually worn him down. These days he felt it was better to keep quiet.

In fact on a few extremely important occasions when he was truly happy it seemed as if she deliberately nagged at him to destroy any sense of happiness he might be feeling. Over the years he had learnt never ever to provoke his wife, that is if he could help it.

Mrs. Amarinder Singh was a big built woman, in fact more than three inches taller than her husband which contributed to the feeling he had of being dominated. To top it all, she wore heels, nothing less than two inches and she would go striding about the place making him feel even smaller. She had piercing brown eyes, sharp features and hair that was cut short in a no nonsense style. She had a strength and energy about her that made others feel tired and along with the stature went an irritating tendency to dominate and interfere. There was a bull dog quality about her, she was almost marnish to look at and she was forever poking her nose in other people's business believing she was meant to solve all their problems. She was a trifle sharp and could be cutting so that everyone including her husband was somewhat scared of her. He thought her altogether too intimidating, disagreeing with her on anything, was a daunting task. She was too outspoken and brusque, with too many sharp edges that poked instead of the softness he had hoped for in his wife. On occasion, she appeared quite ruthless. Although at times whimsical and moody as is generally the case with people who always get their own way, she was basically good at heart and it must be said that she had been a devoted wife but her tendency to nag overruled all else so that not many people got beyond that trait of hers. Once it showed up people were apt to leave her alone. Her constant harping on one subject, her need to disagree and even fight on every issue, had not won her any friends, in fact a lot of people disliked her, the more generous pitied her.

One day Mr. Singh decided to have a dinner party for his office friends and as was usual, in fact de rigueur he asked his wife for her permission. Mrs. Singh eventually agreed but only after a good nag. The preparations were duly made by Mrs. Singh. Of course she had got her way in everything right from the menu to be served to the seating arrangements. She never gave in even on the slightest issue. Each was victory for her. This time they disagreed about the menu, Mr. Singh wanted traditional down-to-earth Indian food; kali dal, dahi vadas and paneer. Food you had to use your hands to eat and doing so the food tasted all the more delicious. His fellow workers would not enjoy or even understand anything fancy. But Mrs. Singh who fancied herself as something of an expet when it came to food wanted a continental style dinner.

Mr. Singh broached the subject one evening after dinner. Mrs. Singh was working on her embroidery, sewing intricate flowers on a table cloth. He stared at the frowning forehead and dark hair in apprehension, heaved a deep sigh and started talking.

– (Husband) Dear.

– (wife) Yes, dear.

– (Husband) Let's have an Indian menu for the party. (Silence)

– Okay? And wouldn't it be nice if we had those scrumptious paneer canapés you excel in.

– (Wife) Yes dear what a good idea.

– Silence

– (Wife) Dear Ami. Indian cuisine is so boring. It is the wrong season for paneer canapés. Milk is so hard to come by and extremely expensive. I'll make some continental dishes, they taste good and are decorative.

– (Husband), wringing his hands in dismay but determined to plod on) Doesn't matter dear, lets still have the Indian. These people won't like anything else. And the paneer. Its not often that we have a party.

– (Wife) All right dear.

– Silence

– (Wife) Dear ...

– (Husband) Yes dear.

– (Wife) None of the people we have invited are fond of paneer canapés and its not really very chic so perhaps we should have something else instead.

– (Husband getting agitated) But Jai, Karan and Monica all like it. I know that for a fact. I want your everyday Indian food. That is what they will enjoy. Not your fancy vol au vents and crème brulee and God knows what else.

– (Wife in an attempt at subdued agreement!) Yes dear.

- Silence
- (Wife) dear ...
- (Husband) How do you know the rest of my colleagues won't like it?
- (Wife) Listen, (throwing down the embroidery), you know the type of people they are. The idea is to impress them so your izzat at work goes up. The more fancy the food the more respect you will command.
- (Husband, meekly sweating and fed up) I'm sure you are right dear, but I still feel ...
- (Wife) Are you dense or what? I keep telling you, for your own sake but it doesn't seem to get through to you.

And it continued till finally poor Mr. Singh would be so worn out he would press his hands over his ears and literally beg his wife to do what she wanted as long as she left him alone.

This was how all the battles were won by Mrs. Singh and lost by Mr. Singh. The end result of any argument was always a foregone conclusion, Mr. Singh would always give in ultimately. Resistance to any idea of Mrs. Singh's was a sure sign that she would make you suffer.

For the next few days before the party Mr. Singh went through hell with Mrs. Singh picking on every idea that was not her own. But finally the day dawned. Mr. Singh was in high spirits, at least the party had not been cancelled and since everything seemed to be going smoothly, Mr. Singh promised himself he would not let Mrs. Singh nag him on any issue and even if she did he would not allow himself to get riled. The best thing was to stay out of her way, with the result that he spent the whole time in the study and let Mrs. Singh get on with the preparations.

Normally this was how Mrs. Singh liked it. However who can really understand the whims and moods of those who fail to understand themselves. And so on this occasion Mrs. Singh did not conform to her usual behaviour and Mr.

Singh's not being present the whole day had put her in a bad mood and gave her a good reason to nag. The moment he admired some arrangement of hers or complimented her on the food, sampling a few snacks here and there, she would have a go at him and she wasn't being verynice about the whole thing. It started from five o'clock when he stepped out of his study and went on till eight o'clock and by which time poor Mr. Singh was a total wreck. And as much as he tried to control it, the nervous twitch was appearing again ... always a bad sign.

While preparing for the dinner party, Mrs. Singh suddenly remembered she had forgotten to put her antique silver candle stands on the table. 'Oh my God', she thought to herself. "They will have to be polished."

"Araminder, Amarinder," she shouted where is the silvo to clean the candlestands? I must do it right now, the guests will be arriving anytime."

At first Mr. Singh refused to answer. He was fed up of hearing her voice. Polishing was normally a job that Mr. Singh did but Mrs. Singh would have a go at it again since it was never up to the mark. But today it had escaped his mind in the urgency of staying out of the way and now he did not feel in the mood to oblige.

"Its lying in the basement," he shouted. "I'm not ready yet, so you will have to do it yourself."

In reply there was a stream of steady abuse interspersed with a nag here and there ... how hard she had worked all day while he sat and did nothing, her yellow and red kanjeevaram sari was sure to get dirty because of his carelessness, her nail polish would get chipped and on and on she went voice trailing as she stomped off downstairs; thump, thump, thump.

"Nag, nag, nag, that's all she ever does," he mumbled. "I wish she would shut up sometimes." As mentioned before, Mr. Singh loved his wife dearly but there was no doubt she exhausted him. He wished he had the guts to stand up to her. Just once, just once he would have loved to teach her a lesson, to really make her beg for mercy. Make her understand the torture it was to have her nag at him everyday. He lay down wearily on the bed. `Better forget about all these wonderful thoughts and have a nap before the guests arrive, otherwise he would be tired and it would present another opportunity for his wife to nag at him; he thought to himself. The deliberate avoidance of his wife over the past few days coupled with the secret exhilaration that the party was actually taking place had left him tense and slightly frayed at the edges. A good nap was definitely needed. He lay down and slept.

When he looked at the watch next an hour had elapsed. He got up guilty. Where was Surinder? The guests would be arriving any minute now. There was not a sound to be heard which was unlike his boisterous wife. He hurried downstairs and looked all over the house shouting her name, Suru, Su ... Where are you? Shouting was something she had expressly forbidden him to do. The kitchen, living room. Perhaps she was snooping in his study. But no, nothing. Then he remembered she had gone to get the silvo from the basement. Oh God, oh my God, he thought in dismay, wringing his hands, I hope nothing has happened. At the same time he remembered the rusty door hinges and the two loose steps he was supposed to fix and had never got round to doing. He hurried down towards the basement his breath coming in jagged spurts, perspiring heavily and listened for a minute against the door when the front door bell rang.

For a long moment he stood motionless. Conflicting emotions could be seen on his face. He put his hand on the door knob and moved to open it but then stopped, his hands remaining on the knob and a moment of indecision seemed to overtake him. Should he ... could he ... would he be able to get away with it? He stood rooted to the spot for several seconds deep in thought.

Finally, he came to a decision. He turned the key in the key hole and put it in his pocket. His hands dropped to his sides and he squared his shoulders resolutely before he hurried upstairs and with a wide smile on his ace he moved towards the entrance to welcome his first guests.

The party was a great success and went on till the early hours of the morning. The food prepared by Mrs. Singh was as usual excellent. And she had been right. The smorgasbord had been especially complimented and although the table was well laden and a veritable cornucopia of food, by the end of the evening it had all but disappeared. The fruit punch that Mr. Singh had liberally laced with a fifteen-year-old-Jamaican rum he had hidden soon had everyone in a merry mood.

Someone had turned on the music halfway through the night and after that there was no stopping the party. In every corner of the house people could be seen gyrating wildly and contorting their bodies into the most extreme positions imaginable. There was a certain joie de vivre, a bonhomie that was prevalent in the air and seemed to touch all.

But there was no doubt that the star of the party was Mr. Singh. He flittered agily from group to group, was a marvellous host and turned out to be a witty raconteur. No one had ever seen him like this before. There was a zestfulness, an abandonment and spontaneity with which he attacked everything. The women hovered around him as he flirted with them all by paying outrageous compliments and of course he danced with an adeptness and verve no one knew he possessed, he least of all! Soon they all wanted to dance with him!

He offered the men the very best cigars (something Mrs. Singh would never had allowed) cracked the dirtiest of jokes and they immediately reversed their impression of him as a namby-pamby and thought the sardar was not such a bad fellow after all.

Of course this metamorphoses had everything to do with the fact that Mrs. Singh was not present. Any questions about her, "where is Suru?" or "I don't see Mrs. Singh" had been smoothly fobbed off and no one was really all that anxious to discover her whereabouts anyway.

As the last of his guests left, Mr. Singh locked the front door and went quietly down to the basement. He put his ear against the door and listened. There was not a sound to be heard. Complete silence. He smiled to himself in satisfaction and went into his study. He sat down in his favourite chair by the corner of the fireplace and lit his pipe. Then he put his feet with his shoes on (sacrilege of the worst kind) on the foot stool and relaxed luxuriantly against the cushions.

What a party he thought to himself, what a party. Everyone had the time of their lives, they were going to be talking about it for some time to come, of that he was sure. No one had wanted to leave they were having such a wonderful time and he hadn't wanted them to go. He couldn't remember when he'd last had such a good time. Why … why … it must have been during his bachelor days, before he had married, before he had met Mrs. Singh! He felt exhilarated. His party was a success, he was a success and many had urged him to have another one soon. Could he? Well, why not he thought to himself. There was no one to stop him how. He smiled gleefully. No one at all.

# 11

# One Night

Suresh awoke with a start and looked around him wildly. He at once realized he must have dozed off to sleep. Where was he … everything looked unfamiliar. He could not place himself. He rubbed his eyes sleepily and peered around once again. It didn't look right. This certainly was not his bedroom. The clock on the wall showed it was three o'clock in the morning. For a moment he started to panic. He looked around the unfamiliar surroundings and then it all came flooding back to him. He remembered everything … every little detail was crystal clear.

He had gone to a local discotheque of questionable repute with some friends. 'The Hideaway' was known as a pick-up place and Suresh had never been there before, he had only heard the wild stories that were a necessary appendage to a place such as this.

The stories always got wilder and seemed somehow unreal but yet they piqued the curiosity and held a strong element of intrigue and fascination for those who had been there. For those who were regulars the spicy stories seemed to rub off on them, so that they acquired an element of temporary notoriety which they reveled in.

He had seen her almost immediately, amidst the flashing strobe lights and the strident music … she stood out. She was surrounded by men, plying her with drinks, their arms and much else all over her, and yet despite her smiling face and loud laughter, she had seemed ill-at-east. She didn't belong and he could sense it.

His first instinct had been to just watch from a distance. But she was like a magnet. She had the kind of lissome body wet dreams were made of and a face that could not be missed. She was beautiful with a soft and vulnerable look that seemed out of place. He could not ignore her. Very much against his will but nevertheless dawn he had asked her for a dance. At first he had thought she might refuse, she looked like she was on the verge of doing so but something in his eyes, something different, perhaps, had made her acquiesce. They had spent the evening together in sensuous abandonment and when the discotheque closed it seemed natural to return with her to wherever she might take him.

He sat up awkwardly in the bed with none of the self-assurance that marked his usual stance and cleared his throat uneasily. His head hurt which was a sure sign he had been drinking again, something he was still not used to. As his senses started to acclimatise themselves, he realized someone was singing in the background but he was in no mood to appreciate the melodious voice, for right at this moment it only served to worsen his growing headache.

"Can you stop that noise?" he said his voice coming out too loudly as he pressed his hands on his head. For a moment there was silence and then he quiet was shattered by the wailing sound of a child.

"See what you've done now," the voice hissed from somewhere in the dark. "Why do you have to talk so loudly? Why don't you just go back to sleep ... or go away?"

And as Suresh's eyes adjusted to the darkness, he made out the figure of a woman who began singing softly again to the wailing child.

"How did I get here?" he asked.

Unexpectedly there was amusement in the voice as she

answered, "you mean you don't know?"

"No", he said in bewilderment.

There was a longer silence where the woman continued busying herself with the child who despite the clucking noises, the soothing motions and singing, refused to go to sleep.

Suresh rose gingerly from the bed and lifted the mosquito netting surrounding him. As he did so two cockroaches fell to the floor. He looked around. The room was terrible. He was in one of the smallest bedrooms he had ever seen with the bed taking up most of the place. There was no other furniture except a large cupboard and table. On top of the table was a ase of magnolias, a riot of pale pink colour, the only bright spark but somehow incongruous in these squalid surroundings.

There was hardly any light in the room making it impossible to discern the darker areas. The stuccoed walls were peeling though some obvious attempt at restoration had been made with the help posters and cheap knick knacks. There were scuttling noises in the corners and he realized with horror the place must be full of rats. The joss sticks burning at one end of the room could not detract from the smell. The room stank of human sweat and had that indefinable look of poverty.

He walked towards the hunched up woman, sitting cross legged, her back towards him, without really knowing what to say and for a moment he just stared as she tried desperately to hide the child from his gaze. But the cloth covering the girl child was totally inadequate; torn and filled with holes, it offered no protection. Staring at the child who looked far too small to him, he asked the first thing that came to his mind.

"Is she ill?" he said solicitously glad to be able to say something, anything to dispel the silence.

She groaned softly. "Yes", she replied sadly. "I have

just not been able to spend much time with her. I never have. I have been too busy trying to earn a few extra rupees," and she added bitterly, "I haven't been able to pay her the right kind of attention. And she seems to know that. Poor child. She's as weary I am. I am a bad mother ... a very bad mother," she added despairingly.

For an hour he watched as she stayed by the child's side, singing softly and feeding her when necessary. Eventually she slept under the mother's constant soothing noises.

She lay the child on a thin mattress, sad and desolate looking and which obviously served as her bed and play pen. Then she got up and moved towards the bed. As she walked, she stumbled slightly. She was tired and at this moment looked it. In a dim light Suresh could see her face. It was a young face but very different without the makeup he had seen earlier. She could be no more than twenty but already the ravages of her profession had left their mark. It looked like a young face that had already seen too much of life. There was a look that was a result of extreme pain, bitterness and a futility that life has only so much to offer and no more. She looked like a young gazelle, proud but almost broken. Awar that it is being stalked and has very little time left.

There was an awkward silence in which Suresh wished a million times that he wasn't there. He cleared his throat noisily and asked in some embarrassment what her name was?

She did not reply. At first he thought she might have gone to sleep. But just when he thought he should ask her again, she answered with a bitter laugh.

"What's in a name? Tara, Jayanti, Neelima, take your pick."

The answer was unexpected and made Suresh feel even more uncomfortable. He could feel himself getting involved. Drawn into another person's life was not what he needed at the moment. Deeper and deeper into the abyss. 'What it buddy boy', he told himself, 'don't let sentiment get the better of you'. He tried to make light of the answer.

"How about your real name?" Again there was silence. After a long while, she answered. "I've forgotten what it was."

This time Suresh had nothing to say. He was momentarily stunned. The blankness of that reply hurt him unexpectedly.

As if sensing his discomfort, she called out to him. He moved forward cautiously. She smiled at him. It was a beautiful smile, beautiful but sad. "Do not let it bother you." And she patted the empty space on the bed beside her. He hesitated and then sat down gingerly. Tenderly she put a hand on his brow and then pulled him down towards her and kissed him. It was perfect. Her lips were soft and her breath smelt faintly of toothpaste and alcohol. Her tongue curved itself around his and sucked gently. She then pushed her tongue against his teeth and next moved it around his mouth, finding all the corners and sending spine-tingling shivers through his body. She then put her hand on his back and moved it up and down in a circular motion. He lifted his leg and put it on her hip.

It was so near heaven, he felt his heart about to burst. He closed his eyes and smelt her presence more keenly. Her skin was soft and sensuous and her caresses become more feverish. She whispered slowly in his ear and then put her tongue inside the cochlea. At once it tickled and excited him and he felt fresh tremors built up in his body. Her body was thin like a reed and moved with sensuous abandon against his. Her long back hair intertwined itself between their bodies in synch with the rhythm of their consent. Her slim arms wrapped themselves around his neck, drawing him even closer and her legs which lay sinuously beneath his, curved their way around his hips. She was graceful, sweet and very intense. She was transformed and any hesitation on his part was swept away in the experience of the moment.

He felt his senses weaken and a delicious sense of lethargy and excitement course through his veins. It was both contradictory and stimulating. He pulled her closer up against his chest and with one began to unbutton her blouse.

Just then the baby started crying. For a moment she stiffened against him and then as if breaking free of something power that held her in its grip, she pushed him away and ran towards the child. She picked her up and started making cooing and soothing sounds while she patted her gently.

Suresh watched her walk up and down the small room for a long while. After what seemed like an awfully long time, the child fell asleep and she gently put her down. Wearily she walked back to the bed. She was exhausted and had almost forgotten about Suresh who was eagerly waiting for her. She looked at his expectant face and wished he would just go away. All she wanted to do was go to sleep. She had been up very early and had a day she wanted to forget about, filled with touch and unsatisfied customers demanding more than she was willing to give and haggling about payment. She had hoped the night would prove more lucrative without any added agro. Why did she always pick the difficult ones? It seemed she would never learn. And here was another weirdo paying to stay the whole night. She should not have agreed. But she desperately needed the money and he didn't look too bad when she had first seen him. But now she wasn't too sure. He wanted the illusion of the real thing. The real thing ... what did he think she was ... an actress? What a pain, what an absolute pain.

Suresh still in the frame of mind she had left him had no inkling of what she was thinking ... Thus when she fell down wearily on the bed, he moved to embrace her lovingly.

But for her the spell of the time before had long been broken and she now turned off the small bedside lamp and submitted herself in silence.

It was a professional execution, dutifully performed. There was no spontaneity, no warmth. It was a paid performance and felt that way. She took her long hair in her hand and in an instant it was transformed into a sensible bun at the nape of her neck. She then removed her clothes with quick, precise movements. The sheer blouse was taken off in a flash, the buttons were loosened halfway down and then simply lifted from the top. The skirt that he had been pushing up her thigh all evening was unzipped and thrown on the floor with nimble fingers and a minimum of fuss. Her undergarments were similarly parted from her body with a quick snap and a slight lifting of her legs. Both were consigned to the heap on the floor. There was no trace of the earlier enthusiasm nor was there any attempt at enticement. She then removed his clothes with the same economy of movement and briskness of manner. Her fingers barely touched his body as she unzipped his pants and removed his shirt. There was no attempt on her part to run her fingers through his hairy chest or down his sinewy muscles. She did ndot look into his eyes at all but concentrated on her task at hand and not a word was spoken between them. He tried to speak. "Not so fast, what's the hurry?" But she simply ignored him and he felt like a fool.

Completely naked, she pushed him down on the bed and sat on top of him. There was no softness and although she went through the right motions, he could sense her distraction and her desire to get the deed over with. Apart from the small incoherent sounds that escaped Suresh's throat and the whisperings that spilled from her mouth with a falseness that was very apparent, nothing else could be heard.

She fell asleep almost immediately but Suresh stayed

awake struggling with his thoughts. He felt cheated and cheap. She had treated him with indifference. As if he were part of a factory that churned out thousands like him. The same bodies, the same desire and all with one thing in mind. Well, what did he expect? He was no different from the countless others who were lying where he was now. Today he was here, tomorrow it would be someone else. Why should she treat him any differently? He hadn't. He had picked her up from the disco as surely as she had known she was being picked. It could so easily have been someone else, any other woman would have done as well just as any other man would have satisfied her requirements. She was simply playing by the rules of the game. Why couldn't he? Yes, why couldn't he? Had his ego been wounded because she hadn't found him attractive enough? Because she hadn't gone into an ecstatic trance over his body or because she could not simulate any kind of passion. He stayed awake wondering where the earlier feeling had disappeared to. He hadn't imagined it or had he? He was no longer sure. If it had been there what had happened? He knew he was being unreasonable. After all what did he expect. A night of love? She was good and had treated him properly. That was all he could expect. When you paid for it that was as far as you got. She barely knew him and she had tried to be nice to him. Only, the poor kid's child had got in the way. He got up knowing he could no longer stay the whole night.

He put his clothes on and moved towards the child. She was fast asleep. She could not be more than two yeas old but already showed promise of great beauty. He felt saddened by her obvious fate. Doomed to follow the life her mother had chosen unless by some quirk of fate she managed to elude its tenacious and destructive grasp. Just as he was turning away, he noticed two huddled figures in the darkness. He was stunned. He had never imagined there was any one else in the room. There had been no noise at all. Had they been there all the time … all the time!? He realized they must have as she had not heard any opening and closing of doors. He felt acutely embarrassed. They must have seen everything. He moved closer. He saw an old couple … who were they … perhaps the girl's parents both desperately trying not to make any noise. They had a stiffness to them that suggested that they had been in this position for quite some time and were patently afraid to move in case they were heard.

He moved towards them trying to say something, anything … in … in anger … in sympathy … what? He was not sure how he felt but they looked very scared. They cowered in fear at his outstretched hand. What were they thinking? Did they think he could hit them? My god he thought, that's exactly what they are thinking. They were terrified. Suresh stopped in his tracks as the old woman began crying and tearfully apologized … for what he thought … for being there, for the noise? "Forgive us, please forgive us. We did not see anything. We did not see anything … Do not punish Tara."

Suresh was appalled. What was wrong with them. What did they think he was … some kind of animal? Obviously. It struck him that on some other occasion, no not just on one occasion, on all the other times Tara had brought a man to the room they had to hide for fear of being discovered. It was certain that their presence was not welcomed on these nocturnal visits and he understood the fear they were going through. They were petrified that he might not pay because of them. And it looked like it wouldn't be the first time that happened.

He moved towards the sleeping girl and peeled some notes out of his wallet and put it by her bedside. Looking at her so young and so beautiful and incredibly vulnerable, he almost forgot himself and wished he could hold her forever in his arms, take care of her and protect her.

But he knew he was in no position to do so. He could not offer any real solution and to even think about it was madness. Where would he take her, how would he support her? His head told him it was simply a momentary feeling, a fleeting sensation. What right had he to uproot her? He shook his head wearily. She seemed reconciled to her life here he told himself, why was he getting so worked up? He didn't know her at all and would in all probability never see her again. Her life, the choices she had made or the choices that were made for her, her fate, these were not his concern. It was none of his business anyway. He took out some more notes and moved away. The door creaked as he opened and she stirred in her bed. "Thank you," she said softly in the darkness. That did nothing to assuage the guilt he was feeling.

"It was nothing", he said knowing full well that he had given much more than he could afford. Now he would have to hitch a ride back home because he had nothing left in his wallet.

He stepped outside. The sun was rising slowly and the sky was that indeterminate colour of orange, yellow and purple that many artists had tried to capture but still remained as elusive as ever. There was a stillness in the air broken by the occasional sounds of the birds warming up to the beauty of another day. In the distance a dog barked. And as he closed the door, he heard the child begin to cry.

# 12

## *Water*

A sleepy village called Pani was jolted out of its lazy complacency and customary lethargy one summer night by a strange and macabre event that took place. Needless to say the village nor its inhabitants were never the same.

Despite the village name, water was the one thing in short supply everywhere. And every year it go worse so that at that moment it was in a particularly perilous state. The villagers spent countless hours debating the issue, and all their free time was taken over by this critical subject. Its scarcity was hard on all but for the women whose duty it was to collect water, it was a lifetime of unceasing hardship.

The women had to walk for hours and days scouring the barren landscape, the dried river beds and the empty wells. They had to compete with roaming animals, marauders and their own kin. All equally desperate and equally thirsty. There was one solitary hand pump in the village that stood out in solitary incongruity. It was rusty and had never been used. It was a continual reminder, a mocking example of what the villagers did not have and of the possibilities that could be.

Other than this black cloud under which the village lived, the people were by and large a sunny lot. They were simple folk who ambled through life, living from day to day with their poverty and hardship but with no malice towards one another. They were one big community. Everyone shared in everyone else's happiness and sorrow. Nobody felt left out and all had a ready-made family to fall back on. Marriages, births and deaths were a village event. If Mina ki ammi had a baby boy, pedas and ladoos were distributed everywhere, if Ramu's kaka got married, the whole village celebrated and if Murli's masi died then everyone grieved. There was a communal feeling of shared responsibilities that had seen them through the tough times and there was a happiness here that was reflected everywhere and in everyone. And because it appeared all enveloping, in a sense almost invincible, everyone accepted it as their right, no different from the landscape which had remained unchanged for centuries.

The village was way off the beaten track, isolated in its natural harshness and devoid of any particularly unique attribute that would endear it to tourists. Thus, it was rarely visited by outsiders. In any election, it was completely overlooked for the simple reason it did not exist on the country's map. It was so indistinguishable, so overlookable that no one knew it existed. And so it remained cut off from the rest of the world.

Until one day ... one day purely by chance, a geography student of no particular brilliance, thumbing through some ancient maps stumbled on its existence quite by accident. And suddenly sleepy village of Pani that no one had heard of for countless centuries suddenly found it was to have a representative living amongst them, an outsider from the capital.

As the most important man in the village, even more important than the village chief, the representative could not be expected to live in just any hut. A big bungalow was to be built for him with all the accountrements of modern living. The most important addition was the water connection he would naturally have. The villagers were ecstatic. If pipes were to be laid for the representative then obviously they too would now have water in the village. And with this in mind they set about building the representative the best bungalow possible.

The process which would normally have taken six months was finished in half the time. The villagers worked hard making sure the work never stopped. Two, three, sometimes four shifts were arranged each day and all the folk contributed in some way or the other. The men dug and sawed and plastered while the women walked miles to get water for the cement. The children and elderly also added their bit, whenever anyone was tired they filled in for a few minutes. As long as the work did not stop, everyone was happy.

Their hard work was rewarded in the beautiful bungalow they built. The walls were covered with intricate hand paintings depicting all the gods and goddesses, the doors and windows were built of the best teak. Old trees that had stood tall and proud were felled in quick succession all for the sake of this man whose presence had changed the village completely. Marble floors and granite bathrooms soon took shape. And the taps were made of pure silver, as they should be. For wasn't that from where the precious water would pour forth?

And finally satisfied with their handiwork and proud of what they had accomplished they agreed that the bungalow was fit for the representative. Word was sent to the capital and soon the representative arrived.

The while village came out to welcome the man who by his very presence, by consenting to come there, had changed the village. They stood out in their best clothes; silk kurta pyjamas, Kanjeevaram and Banarsi saris, in the burning heat with garlands made from the best roses in hand and with numerous thaali's filled with diyas, agarbati, dhup and mithai in abundance; gulab jamun, rasmalai, barfi they were there in every conceivable size and shape to welcome him.

But, the day did not go well right from the start. The representative arrived hours late and drove right past the villages onto the bungalow. They looked at each other in bewilderment but then hurried after the car shouting frantically. Mr. Janardhan Swami jr got out of the car with a dinstinctly supercilious look. He was not amused. More precisely he was in a bad mood. He had not wanted to come to this remote village which no one had been to let alone heard of but he had no choice. He knew it was a step down in his career chart and hardly the promising start of something big as his boss had put it. Who did they think they were kidding? But he knew he could not refuse this posting. If he had not come here it would have meant the end of his career.

The chief of the village attempted to put a huge garland of roses and jasmine around the representative's head shouting enthusiastically, "welcome, welcome". Mr. Swami looked at him with disgust and unceremoniously brushed the garland aside. It fell to the ground in a sorry heap.

"None of that ... that piffle over here", he said, indicating the waiting crowd. "It certainly will not curry any favour with me."

"Are you ...?" He looked him up and down from the corner of his eyes. "Are you the village chief?" Not responding to the Chief's beaming smile and enthusiastic nod, he said tersely, "I want to talk to you," and he moved inside. The headman followed him in as the rest of the villages stared at each other in consternation. They looked at each other in bewilderment and hurt. Why was he so surly? Why could he not even accept their warm welcome? Their hours of preparation had come to naught. Something must be wrong, something must be very wrong.

After a few minutes the Chief came hurrying out. He was no longer smiling. He looked ashen-faced and harried. The villages crowded around him.

What did he say? What did he say? Why is he angry

with us? Have we done something wrong? Tell us what he said. Is he not happy with the bungalow? We can easily change it for him." The questions came at him from all sides. The Chief looked at the villagers' expectant faces, their generosity and desire to please evident in every look and word. He raised his hand in the air to silence them.

"Let us go from here and we will talk later."

The villages all wanted to know what had happened. But the village Chief's word was law and there was no way he was going to say anything if he was not ready. The Chief went to his hut and lay down on his bed with a face like stone. His wife hurried after him. What had happened to him? What had the representative said to him to make him so angry?

She ran into the hut. He looked at her in despair. "What has happened ... what did he say ... what did he say ... answer me?" For a long time he just stared in blankness without saying a word. Finally he let out a string of abuse.

"Bloody fool, who does he think he is, and what does he think we are? Dirt ... nothing ... do you hear he screamed at his wife, "we are nothing, nothing. We are not worthy of the same human kindness that we have bestowed upon him. The representative is a mad man. He wants to make trouble here. And after we have done everything for him." He rose from his chair and moved his hands agitatedly.

"He is ungrateful. He is a bad man. He should not stay here otherwise he will stir up trouble here." He went on ranting and raving. Eventually he stopped pacing and swirled round to look at her. He glared at her, "You know what he said to me ... me ... You want to know what he said to me?"

His wife wondered what he was going to say. He looked as if he was going to be sick. She couldn't deal with another paroxysm.

"He said the villages could not use the water connection. It was for him only. His exact words were that he could not let his privacy be invaded by the village. When I explained the water situation to him, he said he could not shoulder the responsibility. He started throwing all kinds of figures at me. He asked me if I understood how much it had cost the government to build a pipe line for him. They could not add to that already heavy burden by diverting the water for the village. He said water was a precious commodity and the centre could not afford to release water for the entire village. So we must go on as before."

He continued bitterly. "He also said he could not be expected to share his water with the rest of ... the ... the poor, the low life."

"He actually had effrontery to stand there and call us low life and after all we have done for him. After all that we have done for him. What hopes we had, what hopes we had."

"And then you know what else he said?"

"No what did he say?" The words were mere whispers for her throat was dry with fright.

But it did not matter for he did not hear her but went on regardless. "He had the effrontery to say that walking all those miles for water was good exercise for the lazy people. "Good excuse", he hissed. "Can you imagine he called our hard working people lazy? They who have toiled for months for his sake are today dismissed as lazy. Good exercise my foot. Having to go without water for days on end, or walk miles for it is hardly to be seen as an exercise. What we are talking about is our survival and he sees it as ... as ... exercise, nothing!"

"He has destroyed the hopes and trust the people have put in him. There is bound to be trouble. I will have to handle it properly or it could get out of hand. At the village meeting tonight I do not know what I am going to say. What can I say he mumbled to himself. What can I tell the villagers who have lived without water for so long and now when water is within their reach, they are cut off from it by the cruel selfishness of one man." And he put his face in his hands in despair.

She did not know what to say. She had never seen her husband like this. There was no way to comfort him. She dreaded to think what the villages were going to say. They had been working for months on this man's house often leaving their own work, to make sure that everything was done to make his stay as comfortable as humanly possible. And for all their hard work and built up hopes, he had treated them with scant respect and no understanding at all.

She was terribly afraid. She knew her people. They would go berserk when they hard the news. Anything could happen. And in that kind of mood they might even take it out on her husband. What should she do? It was all so unjust.

By the evening she had still not thought of any solution and her husband had not moved from the bed. Silently, she began to cry.

Finally, the time for the meeting arrived. The villagers had gathered in the village square long before the appointed time and were waiting patiently to hear what the Chief had to say. There was an uneasy-calm in the air. It seemed to hold all in its grip and everyone felt the outcome would change the village. But no one could put a voice to it. The air was fraught with tension that was palpably frightening in its intensity.

Finally, the Chief spoke. His voice when it emerged was hard and decision. Completely resolute. There was no feeling or emotion whatsoever. And so he spoke and thus they listened. In those precious moments everything changed, gone forever. They understood that. Each one of them. And the villagers knew that the decision was irrevocable. There was no question that was always the way it had been for centuries and would continue to be so. It was a code that was inviolable. There was never any quorum needed. But this time the chief departed from tradition. Just in case some felt he was doing something wrong or treading the path they were not universally united on, he asked them to step forward and express their views. There was not a single voice of dissent. They were all as one on this issue.

"Fine," he said "then it was decided." The deed would be done tonight itself. There was no need to waste time. And since the outcome would affect the whole village it was unanimously agreed that every man, woman and child would participate.

And indeed they did. Children who were too young were bundled and carried, the old and infirm were similarly assisted, pregnant women were not excluded. And thus, every villager was present, each with the same commitment, collectively resigned to their fate.

That night, the sky was dark. The moon was not visible but covered by the clouds. Not a sound could be heard and not a leaf moved. Even the village dogs whimpered quietly instead of their customary barking. There was a stillness that was frightening. It touched all. An air of expectancy hung like a shroud.

But there was some movement ... quiet and deliberate. Shadows silently glided through. Sometime during the night there was a loud piercing scream ... it tore through the darkness, shattering the silence. It moved from person to person, settling among them. Then there was a calm pervasive silence. Slowly, there was the shuffle of sand being dug followed by thumping and thudding sounds, something was being dragged and then thrown onto the ground. This was followed by more shuffling and the sound of sand against a shovel. And then there was nothing. Nothing, except an ominous silence.

The silence lasted forever. It was ferocious in its intensity and all consuming. Almost phantasmagoric. All the villagers, each and every one of them were its devotees.

Any newcomer who came to the village, having strayed accidentally, soon left. The village had a secret it did not want to share and soon drove outsiders away. Nobody from the Capital bothered to grace the village with their presence and certainly nobody seemed to want to know about the representative they had sent. And so things were left the way they were.

An observant person might notice that for a village which was completely isolated and should by all accounts remain barren, the grass was green and ablaze with all types of flowers. The fruit and vegetables, be it juicy mangoes, luscious ruby red watermelons or burgundy aubergines, were healthy and delicious and the buckets were always full of water.

To be sure it was picturesque. But something was amiss. … There was no more noise to be heard, not a sound. The women no longer sang songs while washing their clothes nor did they have time to gossip with each other. The men did not crack jokes or stop to share a smoke while tilling the land. Gone was the gossip about Sharmaji's wife or Murli's mother, the group discussion on whose cow was whose. All the village magic that had woven its way into everybody's lives had disappeared to be replaced by vapid looks and a general surliness.

Meals were eaten in silence and births, marriages and deaths were organized with as little ceremony as possible. And the children … the children never had time to play any games or indulge in any pranks. No longer was Mala masi's pickle devoured just as she had put it outside the courtyard to marinate. Nor were the village hall windows broken because of some foolish prank or with a longish ball from a cricket game. The children hardly ever laughed and seemed to grow up far too quickly.

Perhaps it had to do with the fact that the elders were in a hurry to pass on a secret …?

# 13

## *Inder and Neera*

It was a warm May morning like any other with the temperature nudging thirty-five degrees and Neera went about her chores with a routine that seemed inborn and had never varied in the past fifty-five years. This was a result of her husband's fastidiousness rather than her own desire for order.

The first thing she did when she awoke at the crack of dawn was to give her husband, Inder his tea. Strong and sugary, the way he liked it and two cups to be precise. And she was always there to pour the second cup which she had learnt he was ready for by a slight noise he made at the back of his throat. He never looked up to acknowledge her presence, that is, except for a mild ruffling of the morning papers which he read without fail.

When Inder went in for his bath, Neera, already bathed and ready, would make his breakfast. Stuffed tomatoes, cheese balls, egg or sometimes a cheese toast which he had begun to like. She was always trying out new recipes to tempt his palate. A glass of cold coffee completed the meal. After having cleared the table and cleaned the dishes with the servant's help, Neera would hurry about the other household chores that never seemed to end and completely filled her day. Like planning lunch, making pickles and jams depending on the time of the year. During the winter she would stock up on carrots and cauliflower, while summer was the time for mangoes and she would spend hours making mango pickles and chutneys, not only for the house but for friends who never bought from the shops but relied on her.

There is no doubt that Neera belonged to the school which believed the husband was an incarnation of god and thus his word was law. He was the supreme being and she the devoted follower brought on this earth to make his life more bearable. And Neera more than believed this. After all she had spent her entire life devoted to her husband asking for nothing in return and getting very little. And so over the years, Inder had grown steadily complacent while taking full advantage of Neera's giving nature.

However, periodically she was overcome with slight feelings of resentment like now. She sighed deeply as she pushed her hair back from her face and stirred the pan. She could feel the sweat trickling down her back, neck and behind her knees. Really, Inder was too much. All he did was read, read, read. He never had anything to say. He never complimented her or even acknowledged what she was doing. He would just grunt noisily. She was sick of those grunts. Was he an animal to grunt like that? He had a voice, well, why didn't he use it? She needed to be appreciated, reassured, to feel that she was wanted. She needed human contact and some inkling that he cared and appreciated what she did for him. When would she be able to sit down and read the papers with someone hovering around her constantly at her beck and call – when, when, when?

The servant Raju, who had been with them for twenty years now looked at Neera sympathetically while washing the dishes. He knew her every mood. She was frowning now over the pan, stirring vigorously and he knew her furrowed brow was not due to concentration but because of the Sahib.

Sahib was different. He was a man of few words and little emotion. He did not like to betray his feelings and kept himself in check. But memsahib was not like that. She wanted more, more than he could give. He felt said sometimes because she was a good woman. She did so much for the Sahib but he took it all for granted. He clucked sympathetically and Neera looked up. She smiled widely trying to dispel her thoughts and not wanted the servant to see how upset she was. He knew all her moods and he saw far too much. And anyway, she thought, it was wrong to think this way. She felt guilty and mentally stuffed the thoughts at the back of her mind.

Neera was a small woman who had over the years become plump. But she had a graceful mien that unknown to her, her husband would revel in from time to time as she went about her household chores. She was the motherly type that people turned to in times of trouble and was always there in the background to support and to nurture.

In contrast, Inder was a big and burly man with a still powerful look that had cowered many in his youth and had only dimmed slightly with age. He was one of those bumptious individuals that no one really liked but people tolerated because of Neera; her warmth, generosity and love were treasured by all. Extremely active in his youth, Inder spent most of the time in the garden, his favourite pastime now that he had retired. His garden was one of the best in the area and indeed he spent all his energy here. He was always to be seen bending and swooping on some plant or the other. Looking to see if the months of hard labour and patients had proved fruitful; digging, planting and watering.

On many occasions he would be so deep in thought that Neera would invariably have to call him across the garden which was spread over several acres. It was beautifully landscaped with wide range of unusual plants and flowers. There was also a vegetable patch which sufficed for their daily needs. When they had bought the place it had created quite a stir and was the envy of those who could not afford one. Farmhouses, as they were called in Delhi, had only come up in the past ten years. With the spiraling land prices and shortage of space more and more people had moved out of central Delhi gobbling up vast amounts of land at what were then throwaway prices. Today the prices were so exorbitant that for the common man it was a dream that would probably not be realized in all his lifetime, while for the very rich it had become a weekend retreat, or winter party place.

Neera looked at the clock. It was time for lunch and there was still no sight of Inder. As was invariably the case, Neera sent the servant to get Inder but when after half an hour there was still no sign of him or the servant she knew she would have to go and get him herself.

As she covered the vast expanse of land she could see him talking animatedly to the servant who kept nodding his head but otherwise looked bewildered. Raju would come back grumbling and she knew exactly what he would say. "He was a cook, meant to spend time in the kitchen cooking and inventing new dishes. He was not meant to dig deep into the ground, dirtying his nails and blistering his hands." Now she would have to pacify him.

Inder was immersed in his latest pastime, digging deep into the ground for the elusive spring water that he believed existed under his earth. Each day he would start out full of enthusiasm, sure that each day was going to be "the day". But as yet it had not happened and Neera was absolutely sure it was not going to happen at all.

"Inder! Inder! Time for much," she declared loudly. She waited for a moment and cocked her ears hoping for a reply but when she heard nothing except the echo of silence, she knew she would have to go and get him physically.

She strolled slowly towards the lawn skirting the vegetable patch and bending to have a look at the bright red tomatoes, the green cucumbers and the burgundy brinjals. Past the enormous Banyan tree, a long time companion and a favourite resting point, past the rosebed with its many coloured hues that she loved, giving an appreciative sniff along the way and up near the edge of the garden. She looked at Inder his tall frame in blue jeans and a T-shirt, his gardening clothes, bent low as he busily dug into the ground. She tiptoed the last few yards and shouted right against his "lunch".

"Oh hmm", he exclaimed in startled amazement at seeing her. "All right I'll be there shortly".

But Neera knew her husband. "Oh no. That's not good enough. Come away right now or else," she said in exasperation and after another five minutes of prodding, he finally acquiesced in not too good humour.

She had noticed that this hole was much bigger than the others and commented on it. "Yes," he said, "I think this time I may be lucky. I can feel itin my bones. There is something different about this patch of earth here" and he moved some loose earth around with his shoe. He mopped his glistening brow suddenly feeling extremely hot and sweaty and rather tired. "Let's go," he said abruptly, "I'm hungry."

That was another grouse Neera held against her husband. He never explained what he was doing and try as she might to get involved or understand anything he did, it always ended in failure. A few terse words was all she could ever get out of him.

If the afternoons Inder slept while Neera busied herself with some knitting, crochet or embroidery. She was always working for the homeless, the under privileged, the poor and downtrodden.

After washing the dishes, Raju came to grumble about the Sahib as she knew he would. She listened to him patiently, even though she had heard it all before and tried to comfort him as she had all these years. "If he left them, what would they do? They relied and trusted him." Raju stared at her in horror. "Leave? Who said anything about leaving? How could she even say it?" His voice shook and a couple of tears were markedly wiped away. "He had been with them for over twenty years, they were like his parents. How could she suggest such a thing? He was insulted. And where did she think he would go? They were his family just as he was theirs." He assured her of his loyalty grumbling that she should understand if he voiced his feelings now and then. After all he was part of the family.

Neera spent another hour consoling him as was the pattern. He had made her feel guilty. But Raju was deeply affronted and it took all her tact to calm him down. By the end of it, she was exhausted and ferverntly wished she could rest but at five o'clock she made a sumptuous tea for Inder who indulged in his two cups. And the once again he was off to his favourite hobby till it was too dark to see in which case he had to stop and come into the house.

It was in the midst of this monotonous regularity and the humdrum existence of daily living that Akash entered. (That is what she decided to call him – a gift from the skies). A small slight lad with no remarkable qualities that distinguished him from the ordinary or possessed with any good looks that would elevate him above the hoi polloi. He was a scrawny gangly lad of twelve with huge eyes and sharp features. He was brusque when spoken to but for the most part remained silent. There was nothing endearing about hum but he ignited some maternal spark in Neera. Right from the beginning they seemed to have an invisible rapport that was alien to others. He took to appearing during the day around lunch time and then after being given some food would disappear.

Inder did not pay the boy much attention but Neera was obsessed. Being childless, her whole life had been devoted to looking after Inder who not being the most sensitive of men had never really acknowledged her as a person with whims and desires ofherown or her individuality as a person. He accepted that once married to him she would spend her life looking after him which she did admirably and he had to acknowledge he had no complaints on that score.

But unknown to him, Neera did. Suppressed of all her longings, and devoid of children she had hidden her inner self from Inder realizing he was not the kind of person to whom she could really open up. He had never been a demonstrative person and very early on in their marriage she had learnt to make do with little. But here was someone out of his orbit who actually needed her. Akash would wait patiently for her when she was not at home and even refused to eat the food the servants had been told to give him in her absence. He depended on her perhaps as Inder did but also gave in return some kind of show of dependence, some affection, something which Inder had never done.

The child had arrived from nowhere. Enquiries had elicited no response and finally Neera decided she would keep him with her permanently.

Inder of course threw a fuse. "What absolute drivel. Him and here?" he said incredulously looking at the placid child who never seemed to speak, he often wondered how Neera conversed with him. He always seemed to be looking at Inder and passing judgement on him. There was a veiled expression about the eyes, he always masked his thoughts and he had a look of contempt, Inder thought, that was always directed towards him. It was as if the boy thought he was no good, certainly not good enough for Neera.

"Just imagine! A little pipsqueak of a boy thinking

about him such a manner and not even bothering to conceal his thoughts." Neera of course could never see it. "You are being imaginative," she said in one of her rare moments of exasperation. "I want to keep the child, he is a good boy who desperately needs love and affection. He's been starved of both. He has nowhere to go and we can afford to do this good deed."

In any fight between the two Inder was invariably the winner. He could be extremely mulish and Neera neither had the spirit nor the longing to win. But this was different. For the first time Inder had an opponent of equal if not more strength. Neera was determined to fight for Akash if need be. He stirred in her suppressed longings of motherhood that having finally been lit again after all these years she was not about to let go so easily. In the event Inder displayed rare perspicacity. Perhaps he realized that this once she was willing to stand up against him and eventually gave in but with no attempt at grace. And with some show of authority and the strong admonition that she was to keep the little rapscallion out of his way and his living with them should in no way disrupt their lives.

But that's exactly what did happen. Neera had time only for Akash. No longer were meals given on time, nor were shirts ironed the way they used to be. Morning tea, a sacrosanct ritual for over thirty years had failed to materialize one morning after numerous late starts. One day, however, it got too much for Inder as he saw the clothes laid out for him. "Forget being properly starched," he said to himself, "these are totally mismatched and the colours are dreadful." Inder wore conventional clothes that were always soberly coordinated. He had firm ideas about what went with what and would not move at all. New fashions did not find favour with him. And bright colours were anathema to him. "Has the woman gone mad?" he said picking up the bright blue shirt that was party wear and had been matched with a yellow pair of trousers he had never worn before and brown socks. Brown socks! He pushed the clothes aside with disgust. And sat down heavily on the bed. This was too much. Neera had gone too far and must be stopped before she went totally berserk.

"Neera," he roared. "Where are you, woman? Come here at once."

At first Neera did not hear. She was far away on the sand heap playing with Akash. The servant, Raju, on hearing Inder yelling hurried outside to get her. But Neera seemed to be in a world of her own.

"What is it?" she said coolly, unconcerned by the servant's flustered appearance who in all his years at the house had never seen the Sahib in such a rage. "Its sahib," he muttered agitatedly, "he's gone mad, screaming for you." "Well tell him I'll be along shortly", said Neera smiling sweetly at Akash who looked at her contentedly and went back to playing.

The strange thing was that Neera did not run back to the house on hearing Inder was looking for as she normally did nor did the fact that he was screaming in a totally uncharacteristic manner upset her. In fact if the truth be known it did not seem to affect her at all. And if one looked closely they would have noticed a quiet though definite change about her. The slight apprehensiveness and the servile attitude that seemed to be a part of her personality had all but disappeared to be replaced instead by a certain determination and resolve that showed in her eyes. Of course, Inder had never bothered to look into her eyes and would definitely not have noticed the change.

Eventually, Inder had to come out to the lawn puffing with anger. "Why are you shouting Inder?" she asked quite unruffled.

He stared at her and rubbed his eyes as if he could not quite believe himself. The truth was he was taken aback. Her answering him and remaining so calm in the face of his rage was unlike the Neera of old. It was so out of character, not so much the question itself as the manner in which it was asked. He could not quite believe it. That she actually had the temerity to question him was unheard of.

"The child must go", he expostulated vigorously. He is a menace and nuisance to this house. I told you in the beginning that he could stay as long as he didn't disrupt my life. But he's turned the whole place upside down." "And look at you," he said unkindly. "Just look at you. You've become totally senile about him. You can't seem to function unless he's around. Get a grip on yourself, woman. He is not your child, you must remember that, he's a vagabond who'll disappear one day, the same way he arrived. Better get used to that. For your own good."

In the face of this verbal onslaught, Neera betrayed no emotion whatsoever. She simply let him rage on for the next five minutes and then when he had finally run out of steam, she just smiled her gentle smile and said nonchalantly that it would all work itself out and he was not to fret so.

And true to her word everything fell back into place. Over the next few days there was a perceptible difference in Neera's attitude and the household once again hummed with its usual efficiency. Tea was once again given on time, strong and sugary just as he liked it, the shirts were properly starched and placed in matching sets every morning and Neera herself seemed to be always there when needed. He only had to rustle his paper and another cup of tea was served, a cough would signal that he wanted a second helping of food or his frown would warn her not to continue talking about a topic he did not want to pursue. It seemed like the brief aberration had never occurred. The only irritant was the child whose presence continued to irritate Inder. He was always around and Neera's continuing pampering irked him sorely. But he thought in triumph, I am the victor, I am the one who has the real say. I am the master of the house and Neera would not dare disobey me. Reassured, he would often look at the child and smile gloatingly. Akash would simply stare back with those strangely penetrating eyes that always gave him the creeps.

And thus the years rolled by. The daily routine continued as usual. Looking into the garden from the outside, passersby would often see Akash and Neera playing together and eventually Inder was not visible at all. Except for his clothes that were regularly despatched to the dhobi, his morning papers that were delivered extra early or the tea being made there was no visible sign of him. He was no longer seen taking his daily walks or tending to his plants. It was as if he had disappeared into thin air.

Meanwhile the garden blossomed. Amidst the flowers various mounds of differing sizes could be seen dotted all over the landscape. These were Inder's holes that he had dug deep into the ground hoping to find the spring he believed was nestled below. The larger hole he had been excited about had finally been filled. It stood out from the rest because of its size but also because of its beauty. It was covered with all kinds of flowers; mimosa, iris, hyacinth, geranium, daphne - that would have made Inder proud. Often Akash could be seen standing over it eyes veiled with a strange and inscrutable smile on his face.

# 14

# The Flip Side

Mrinalini arrived in Delhi from the US one bright October morning. It was hot but there was a slight breeze in the air that prevented the sun from becoming too overpowering. It was also a pleasant time of the year. The torrid heat of the previous months was melting away and in its place was the promise of a gentler winter awaited with much anticipation by Delhi people. The trees would be lush with greenery and the flowers would bloom in all their glory, their vivid colours sprouting everywhere, in the gardens and in vases that transformed the very atmosphere. A time of transition, certainly a time of new beginnings.

Mrinalini was thirty years old and the pride and joy of her family. Their whole world revolved around her whims, and fantasies. When she was happy the household moved smoothly and everyone went about with beatific smiles on their faces. When she was not, an uneasiness lay upon the household that could only be dispelled with her laughter. They loved her unreservedly.

She was as independent as they came pursuing whatever interest took her fancy. And whatever she did she excelled at. No matter how trivial or how mundane an accomplishment it was treated with such reverence, such love, it made her totally confident about everything she did and she grew up to be one of those individuals who is rarely troubled with self doubt.

The only time she had resisted her parents was when she refused to marry at an age when "all good Indian girls got married." They had to admit they had not pushed her too hard always saying there was no rush and it would happen next time ... next month ... next year. But all too soon the years slipped by so that even her parents had given up on her not to mention the several friends and family who had used their prowess to matchmake to no avail and had prohesised she would forever remain on the shelf and die a spinster.

Imagine then her parents delight at the announcement of her wedding. They were told at three o'clock in the morning with typical Mrinalini drama. The news was greeted with a mixture of disbelief and great thankfulness. Initial worry had soon been replaced by joy and not too much reasoning or questioning into the whys and hows of the situation. It was happening and that was good enough.

Time passed quickly. The wedding was over before Mrinalini could grasp the realities of the situation and her parents left a few days later. Thus Mrinalini was left to settle down to her new life.

Below are the letters that Mrinalini would have written to her parents. However, they never reeived them for she invariably tore them up.

DECEMBER 23

Hope this letter finds you both in the pink health. As for me I am perfectly fine and not mention quite delirious, you know it is only one months since we have been married and I am still living in another world. Everything seems unreal and sometimes I have to pinch myself to make sure it is not a dream.

I miss you all dreadfully but Amit is very good to me and indulges my every whim. Yesterday we were talking about life back home and I happened to mention to him how we used to just pack ourselves in the car and go away for weekends and the fact that I miss not being able to do it here because he works on Saturdays as well. Well, you cannot imagine what he did, you just cannot … today he says he's made arrangements to go to Agra to see the Taj Mahal. He says, "if you have not seen the Taj Mahal then you are not a true Indian," and he wants me to see it in the moonlight. We will stay at the famed Maurya Sheraton. Isn't that wonderful? It was so unexpected. Isn't he so romantic? I can't believe my good fortune. My mother-in-law on hearing the news said, "someone likes the good things in life." Everyone laughed but I let it pass. What is the point? It would only create tension. But what I wonder is why she felt she had to make such anasty remark? It was so uncalled for.

We have so many servants in the house but yet my mother-in-law keeps cribbing that I don't do any work. That I have it too easy. She is always making some comment or the other about me and the sly innuendo is so spiteful.

Life here in India is very different. One doesn't realize it when you come on a holiday because you are simply intent on having a good time and not delving too deep beneath the surface. Most people are extremely conventional and have strict codes that need to be adhered to.

Amit usually comes home late. My heart beats every time I hear his car coming up the driveway and I feel like running towards him but I have learnt to restrain myself and wait patiently till he comes to the room. That is after he has gone to is parents' room and greeted them and then his elder brother's room. He does this every day!

At times I must admit I find it extremely hard going. On one occasion, I just could not help it and I ran towards the door without thinking. But I don't think I would ever do it again. Everyone, with the exception of Amit, gave me the strangest looks and I think even he felt slightly uncomfortable. Adapting to a completely different lifestyle can sometimes be traumatic as one has such a different set of responses.

JANUARY 1

I want to wish you a very happy New Year. What did you do ... how did you celebrate? I want you to tell me all the details ... the hugs and smiles, the laughter and joking ... everything so I can feel as if I were there.

Yesterday I got into a bitter argument with my mother-in-law. She had spent the entire evening praising the daughter-in-law of one of her friends. "The best possible daughter-in-law one could hope for; respectful, dutiful and obedient. She is so lucky ... so lucky." And meaningful glances were thrown in my direction!

I could not resist the obvious dig and asked her what she meant by "obedient and dutiful?" Amit was also there and as is becoming more and more the norm, gave me look of warning which clearly said "shut up."

However, there is only so much I can take. With one of her artificially contrived looks of hurt which she has practiced to perfection, my mother-in-law said "You go gallivanting all over town and I never stop you. I never interfere and question where you are going or why you come back late."

I replied, "I am thirty years old, why should I tell you every detail? And its not true to say I don't tell you where I am going. I do. But you pretend not to hear me. And moreover, your son does not leave the house without telling you where we are going to be." I couldn't really understand what this conversation had to do with being dutiful and obedient, though!

JANUARY 12

How is everything? It is still very cold over here and I cannot get used to it despite the fact that temperatures are not lower than eight degrees Celcius. But because there is no central heating, I can feel the cold in my very bones. But not to worry, I just ply myself with more woollies of which, as you well know, I have an abundance. Thank god for all those shopping sprees!

Amit is fine. He is working very hard so that perhaps we can come and visit you later in the year. Wouldn't that be absolutely great? I have already started shopping around for the cheapest air fares and am sure I am driving the travel agents made with my persistent enquiries. I just hope prices don't go up too much.

Had another bout with my mother-in-law which is becoming something of a regular feature. The other day she told Amit I don't greet her properly and am rude to her. I do greet her but either she pretends not to hear or she has a genuine hearing problem. In which case she should definitely see a doctor. Should I offer to take her to one? I'm sorry. That was a bad joke.

FEBRUARY 2

Greetings. I know you must be very angry with me for not having written since the 12th, but I have been extremely busy – I have decided to look for a job. Sitting in the house is just not my kind of thing. So I am doing the rounds at the moment. Getting a job is a bit different here. Despite the presence of the multinationals and the increase in the variety of jobs, you still have to go through someone who knows someone, who knows someone. Once you are in, well then it is up to you. But getting there is the hurdle. I'll keep you posted.

My mother-in-law can be amazingly cruel, whether its intentional or not is another matter though I believe it is the former. She keeps harping on what dowry other boys got in their marriages. She says those who do not have to give dowries are very lucky – like me I suppose? Then she goes on about how Amit was flooded with offers but he chose me and they accepted his decision. At the time I had thought it was the principle of the thing that mattered to them. If I had known that I would have to be grateful all my life, I am not so sure I would have married him.

I miss you both so much I cannot express it in words. I wish I could come home for a short time. I am keeping my fingers crossed.

APRIL 6

I am feeling extremely low today.

As I live here I learn more about everyone even my own husband. He has such good qualities. But he is just a little bit of a coward, too much of a mother's boy.

For instance, we discuss things in private and come to some kind of agreement but when he is with his parents he forgets about what we had discussed and follows their point of view completely. At first, I didn't think too much of it and even put it down to my being so sensitive, reading too much into everything. But I realize it is a big drawback I will have to live with. There is no other way to express it. My husband has no backbone.

When we first met, it felt right to be together, to imagine that it would always be so. I was attracted by his gentleness and sensitivity. He seemed to understand me so completely that it immediately set him apart from others. In short, I was completely disarmed. I thought this was going to be one of those marriages where we were equals, we would share in each other's dreams, support one another. We would be friends as well as lovers.

And that is how I started my married life secure in the knowledge that these dreams would bear fruition. They have not. Amit never protests with his parents about anything. Whatever they say is right and whatever I say is somehow, not wrong, but of less importance. So that my views can be and should be easy to change or to overlook.

He says, "I am too sensitive and don't understand. I must learn to compromise." He says, "I am too imaginative and live in another world." Isn't that what he loved about me in the first place? Whenever I complain to him about anything, he laughs it off saying, "it is nothing." He says, "if it doesn't bother him why should it bother me?"

Isn't that a stupid and insensitive answer? I am truly surprised at him, sometimes he seems like another person. A stranger, not the man I had thought I had married. Do you think that is the problem? That I thought I was marrying someone who only existed as a figment in my imagination? Why doesn't he ever say anything? Does he keep quiet to maintain the peace in the house or does he genuinely not care?

My mother-in-law is playing a new game these days. She makes nasty remarks all day and when I tell Amit and he confronts her, she lies. She denies the whole thing and now Amit thinks I invent things. She never actually says anything too vindictive in his presence so he does not have any real evidence.

APRIL 8

I have some great news for you. I have got a job – finally. It's a teaching job at the university. Isn't that great? I'll start next week. I'm really glad because it will keep me busy during the day and out of my mother-in-law's hair for most of the time. But the main thing is that I want to do this – so here goes. Wish me luck because I am extremely nervous.

MAY 12

You don't know what a joy it was to read your letter. I knew you would be delighted about the job. It is going along very well so far and I am loving every minute of it. I can't understand how I stayed at home all this time. I couldn't do it now.

The timings are very good because I only have four lectures a day. So, I am usually back home by five-thirty or six. The students actually seem to like me. I was afraid I would have problems with them, especially with my accent, but so far they have all been very cooperative. The first few lectures were tough–my voice actually squeaked–but I am more confident now.

Although I am enjoying the work and the load is not too heavy, I have to admit it is quite tiring. The other day I came home late from work and decided not to go out to a party that was being held that evening. Well, my mother-in-law could not let it pass. She said, "no one pushed you into taking a job. What will people say when you don't show up at the party? They will say we are making our bahu work too hard. Actually we all know you live like a Maharani!"

That really got me mad. I counted to ten like you always told me, then said, "I try to help you as much as possible even though you don't really like it nor need it. You have more than enough servants to do your bidding but you just hate to see me not doing anything. I always go everywhere you want me to and it is just that today I am extremely tired. Nothing will happen if I don't go."

By now everyone had come into the room. There was dead silence. She seemed taken back. For a few minutes she seemed at a loss for words. But when she realized she had a full audience, she came into her own. "You are insolent and rude. You have no time for the house, me, let alone my son." I thought Amit would at once rush to my defence. But although I gave him a look of desperate appeal, he did not seem to see it or chose not to, for he remained silent.

After another pause, she said, "you should count yourself lucky to have a mother-in-law like me. (sic)

She went on for quite a while. No one else had anything to say and I was too exhausted and sick of the whole shenanigans by the end of it to say anything further.
What is happening – my whole life seems to be falling apart.

JULY 1

Yesterday Amit and I had a major row. They are becoming increasingly frequent these days. He said, "I exaggerated everything and also invented half the things his mother never actually said to me!" Can you imagine that? Me, lying! I cannot stand it. Amit openly taking his mother's side. He says, "if his mother criticizes me, she does so because I deserve it."

SEPTEMBER 15

We went to Goa for a few days. Amit had some work and his flight and hotel were paid for. I went along and paid for my ticket out of my own money. I also had to hear a lot of nasty remarks till the time I left. But it was worth it just to get away. I had a great time lying on the beach and just drifting ... drifting. The peace and tranquility was just what I needed.

OCTOBER 20

Before you get ready to scold me for not writing let me tell you the good news. No, I am not pregnant but I think I will be coming home soon. I have almost got the full amount for the ticket saved.

Had another fight with Amit. He said, "If I cannot adapt myself here, I should perhaps go back home." I could not believe it. How did he change so much? Or had he always been like this and I had never seen it? He says, "I am always cribbing." But who else should I turn to if not my own husband? He doesn't want to listen. As I think back I realize when we married we really did not know each other. We were still at the stage where our surroundings and lifestyle had not impinged on us. We had never argued but then why should we have, there was nothing to argue about? He said, "I hardly talked before we got married and look at me now. I cannot seem to stop talking and about all the things he does not want to hear."

Well, what did he want? What had he married me for? When we got married did he ever dream that life would degenerate so fast? I think not. Neither of us realised what we were getting in to. It must be difficult to live under the shadow of your parents and never emerge as a person in your own right. But he had known that. Had he deliberately ignored it and closed his eyes to reason? But, he knew how things were now, why didn't he do anything about it? Where were all the dreams we had hoped for, would any of them ever come true.

### November 7

I feel totally confused. My in-laws act as if they do not like me. They treat me with indifference which is worse than anything else. They never bother to chat with me the way you folks did, to enquire about my job and generally about my life. I know in-laws can never replace your own parents but surely they can try.

You, my parents used to sit with me for hours and talk. You would listen to everything, no matter how trivial. You were excited as I was by my successes and depressed when you saw me down. Of course there were times when we argued, who didn't? But most of all I knew you were there for me.

Can one never have good relations with one's in-laws? God knows I have tried. But they never manage to see beyond the petty little incidents that soon become major power struggles. They have a daughter who is also married. I am sure they could not envisage her in the state I am in now.

### December 1

Life is pretty hellish these days. They are filled with taunts and jibes and sly innuendoes that initially hurt like hell but then you gradually learn to live with it like everything else. And without love. For where was the love Amit and I thought we had? There seemed no trace of it now in the squalid pettiness that our life has degenerated into. I had not chosen this way of life any more than Amit had. We could not imagine that this was what marriage was all about. I had always believed I was above the rest. My marriage would be different, different from those other marriages that others were condemned to live with for the rest of their lives. I, of course, would have something else, a marriage based on rights, where I would stand up for my rights with the man I loved by my side defending me to the end.

How naïve and idealistic it all sounds.

The enlightened family I had married into were not as enlightened as I imagined. The veneer went only so deep and no more. There is a great sadness in me as I realize that I can hange none of it. To be honest, I no longer have the motivation that drove me a year ago. Amit accepts everything. But I can not. By accepting their prejudiced, vicious and narrow views, I am snuffing out my own individuality. Surely that has to mean something? Well, it certainly means something to me. No, I can not live like this day after day. Why should I and for whom? Certainly not for myself.

And if I can not accept, if I can not bow to their ways then the only alternative is to leave. What would they say? I can just see my mother-in-law's reaction. She would smile in triumph and though feigning great distress would manage to get the message across that she had always known. "My type would never make a suitable bahu."

My father-in-law would simply retreat further into the isolated cocoon he wraps himself in and probably not deign to answer because he thinks he is so superior and his ego would not allow it. And Amit. The man I had left another continent, another way of life for? The man I thought I would live with always, growing old together. What would he think?

The usual I suppose. The utterly predictable from a man I once thought was unlike any other. He would answer in a totally expected form. "Why can't you get on with them?

They don't interfere with you, they hardly say anything to you. Do they ill treat you, do they stop you from doing whatever it is you want?" The answer to all that is of course, `no'.

Ever since I got married, I have been plagued by doubts and self doubts, something which is completely alien to my nature. I thought that since I had chosen this life, I would have to live with it. But no more. I have made by decision. I have decided to leave Amit. What is the point of carrying on in a marriage that is a farce? If I am honest with myself, I have lost respect for him. If only he had stood by me for me. But he has not and I must continue with my life as I see fit.

I know I have it in me to forge a new life for myself. To stay here is to surrender, to admit defeat and no matter what, my life has to mean more than that.

DECEMBER 7

Thank you for the tickets and your generosity. You should not have done it. I know you sent it to your daughter whom you love and for no other reason. But for my in-laws it was just another instance of the way the "bahu's family should behave … by giving, giving and more giving."

DECEMBER 20

Two days before Mrinalini was supposed to reach her parents, a telegram arrives at their house.
'Regret … stop … the said and ultimely death of … stop … beloved bahu … Mrinalini … Cremation will take place on $20^{th}$ … stop.'